ASHLEY BEEGAN

The Holiday Home

D1521970

First edition

Editing by Three Owls Editing

This book was professionally typeset on Reedsy.
Find out more at reedsy.com

Dedicated to Cally,

Thank you for teaching me what true friendship is.

xxx

Contents

Prologue

T he sound of footsteps made Simone Johnson freeze mid-step. She turned her head so abruptly that her thick, black glasses slid to the end of her nose. An involuntary shiver ran through her as she listened to the darkness. The thin jacket on her arms was useless, but the October night was much colder than expected considering it was still autumn. She may as well have not bothered wearing a jacket.

It was close to midnight, but she could still hear the faint sound of traffic from the incessantly busy A52 that led from her small city of Derby to the adjacent Nottingham. She eyed the street behind her for a moment. No dark figures hid anywhere. And there were no more footsteps. The darkness was playing with her mind. It was probably her own footsteps echoing off the tall buildings. She shook her head and continued to walk.

Staying out so late was a stupid idea. It was fine walking alone in the city centre where life still buzzed and plenty of people filled the streets, moving from pub to pub and enjoying their nights out. But away from the drunken hubbub the streets quietened quickly, and the only other movements were flickering shadows which did not belong to her.

Drinking with the work girls was hardly her idea of fun,

anyway. The first hour was OK, but she should have left after that second vodka as originally planned. Jenny was so damn insistent. Being the boss, she was hard to say no to. In true Jenny Grey style, she'd bought shots for the entire team within an hour of entering the first pub. You'd never guess she was in her fifties with the way she acted. Even now, Simone could smell the whiff of Jäger on her jacket from the attempt to chuck it away before anyone saw. Most went on the sticky, carpeted floor, but some did spill on her arm in her haste. Luckily, she was quick enough, and no one noticed.

Other than that man who'd smiled at her from the bar. She'd given him a look which told him she wasn't interested in no uncertain terms. That was the last thing she needed right now. People are strange with alcohol. There aren't any other situations in life where it's socially acceptable to be *that* pushy about doing something you don't want to do.

She approached the alley behind her flat and glanced behind her once more to make sure it was safe to enter alone. She fingered the set of keys in her hand and pulled the thin jacket tighter around her shoulders. The street was still empty, but the feeling of being watched stayed with her.

She chewed on her lip, stalling the moment she'd have to enter the alley. But she'd have to walk through it whether she felt safe or not. It lay in between two high-rise buildings, and her flat was at the end.

It was a one-minute walk. She could hardly get a taxi at such a short distance. Even getting a taxi from the pub was laughable. It was less than ten minutes to walk home from where they'd been drinking. She gripped the set of keys in her right fist and entered the alley. The largest key poked out between her fingers like a weapon. Useless, really, but it gave a speck of confidence nonetheless.

She took quick steps, but it took only seconds to hear the heavy footsteps again, and she knew straight away they were not her own. Whoever was behind her was rushing now and made no effort to keep up with the fall of her own footsteps.

Her heart thumped in her chest. She picked up her pace and glanced behind her, praying to see no one there. Or at least let the stalker be female so she stood a chance at getting away unscathed. But the dark figure behind her was far too tall for that to be likely.

She should have screamed. Or ran. Anything would have been better than freezing. But her body wouldn't listen to her brain screaming at it to 'move.' Her mouth was dry, lips stuck together and unable to form words or even a pitiful shout. She urged her legs to move, but they were a dead weight as if they were a magnet to the ground.

It happened in slow motion, yet before she'd considered what to do he was upon her. He pinned her arms against the wall and her useless weapon of keys fell from her hand.

She tried again to make her dry lips form a scream, but a sharp pain in her stomach took her breath away. She tried to double over to breathe, but he pinned her heavily to the wall. Something sharp was against her throat.

"Don't fucking move," he spat, his voice low and gruff.

The hard bricks of the wall behind dug into her skin as he shoved her hard against it. Yet she forced her head backwards against them so she could face him, determined to see what she could of her attacker. A black balaclava covered his face. All she could see were his eyes and their magnificent sharp blue that pierced her own. They were the ice-cold eyes of a killer.

That was all the motivation she needed to get her body connected to her mind. She raised a knee with all her might and belted him in the stomach. He groaned and doubled over, but his grip on her throat tightened.

She brought up her leg to knee him again, but he'd grown wise and he caught her leg mid-strike. He twisted his body and threw her to the ground.

The sharp gravel of the dirty alley floor scratched her face as she landed, but she sucked in deep breaths of air whilst scrambling to her knees. Thank God her legs were working.

But his foot got to her face before she could turn around. Her nose and lip exploded in pain like she'd never felt before. She cried out in agony and the noise shook her. Her lips were working again.

"Fire!" she screamed.

He punished her with another kick straight to the chest, and she fell back on the ground taking in more gasps of air. It was getting more difficult to breathe with each kick. As she struggled, he climbed on top of her and straddled her chest. Her arm flew out and smacked him in the lip. He grunted in pain and grabbed both of her flailing arms, forcing them down under his knees.

He stroked her cheek with the sharp tip of the knife as she shook and gasped for air. Blood seeped from his lip. At least she smacked him good before he ended her life. He put one hand around her throat and raised the knife high in the air.

"No four weeks for you," he growled.

She tried to cry out but was too winded to form anything other than a splutter. He brought his hand down with such force she knew she would never survive and closed her eyes tight to wait for the pain. No one was around to save her.

Nobody would care anyway, apart from Kerry Oakland.

But the pain never came. The knife clattered to the ground beside her and his weight disappeared. Her eyes flew open and wildly searched the alley, but he was gone. Her hands scrambled against the gravel of the hard ground, trying to find something to grab onto to help her sore body stand. She pushed herself against the wall, searching up and down the alley for her attacker.

Loud voices came from the opposite side of the alley, towards her flat. Men's voices. They must have spooked him. She rubbed the tears from cheeks and pushed herself up from the floor to stand. She needed to get the men's attention, but something shone in the weak light and caught her eye.

The knife was in the middle of the alley.

She scrambled over to it and grabbed it. It was a large knife with a curved wooden handle. She fingered the sharp blade, running her fingers along the serrated edge. Holding the knife made her much calmer.

"Fire!" She screamed the word her father always told her to use in an emergency. He always said people are too scared for their own safety if you scream for help, but they come running for a fire. She heard the men shout and footsteps coming towards her.

She picked up the knife and brought it down hard on her thigh. The pain felt as though someone had torn her skin off with bare hands and grabbed hold of her insides, squeezing her flesh, muscle, and bone. Her leg shook, and she felt faint as she looked down at the knife. The alley grew dull, and everything faded as she slipped into the darkness.

Simone

Sitting on the hard tiles of the kitchen floor made the lower half of Simone's body grow numb. She stretched out her right leg to regain some blood flow, but didn't let her gaze wander away from the front door of her flat. She nestled further into the corner of the kitchen units. It wasn't exactly comfortable with the handle of the drawer sticking into her neck. But she ignored it. It was a small price to pay to stay alive. Christmas was a month away. Maybe she'd last until then and get to have her peaceful Christmas Day to herself as usual.

Her eyes stung from not daring to blink. She squeezed them closed and opened them again as quickly as she could. Her ears strained for any noise in the corridor outside the flat. Every time a neighbour came, her fear flared and she raised the carving knife; keeping it steady in her hand. It had been four weeks since the man with the icy blue eyes attacked her, and she was fully healed from the cuts and bruises he inflicted. Though her thigh would take longer to heal as she'd cut the muscle. Well, *he* had cut the muscle, according to the police report.

No four weeks for you.

The gruff words had bounced around in her head since the

night of the attack. Meaning his voice was still fresh even though a month had passed. Hardly surprising, since she also heard it in her dreams most nights. She should have healed over the last month mentally too, as memories faded, but instead her anxiety increased tenfold. As if it wasn't bad enough before this stranger attacked and almost murdered her. At least Jenny had given her a month off work. Though she was due back in two days.

No four weeks for you.

If she survived tonight, that is. On a normal Friday night, she'd either wrap up in a blanket watching some sort of true crime documentary, or allow Jenny to drag her to the pub. The blanket was preferable, though it was good to appear socially normal sometimes. Whatever normal meant. Yet tonight she was alone and sitting on the floor in silence, waiting to see if *he* was going to pull at her door handle. Sometimes her eyes wandered away from the door, but she immediately pulled them back. She quickly checked the clock above the door. It was half past seven, and the November sky was dark already.

There was no proof that he was going to come for her, but Simone would not end up like those other girls. There was only one thing she could think he was referring by 'four weeks'. And that was the Lunar Killer. A serial killer who terrorised Derby a couple of years previously, beating young women up, befriending them and murdering them four weeks later. Which was why she was now watching the door to her flat, even though the police caught the Lunar Killer two years ago and locked him away.

Something tickled her thigh, and her hand flew to her chest; but it was just her phone vibrating. She let out a breath. Is this really what that scumbag had reduced her to? She really needed to get a grip. She pulled it out of her jeans pocket to see who was calling – a withheld number. But she knew who that would be.

"Hi, DI Swanson," she answered.

"Hi, Simone. How are you?" Detective Inspector Alex Swanson asked in his serious voice. He was one of the leading officers investigating her attack, and the first one she'd told her story to. A very stoical, lumberjack type of man she'd never seen laugh. He took everything she said with absolute solemnity.

She plastered a fake smile on her face to make lying easier. A slogan from a previous call centre job flashed in her mind; *'smile when you dial'.*

"I'm absolutely fine," she replied.

DI Swanson had also expressed concern about what the man meant by 'no four weeks for you.' But Simone refused any sort of protection he offered. She couldn't stand the thought of police officers being inside the flat with her. It was her home. A sanctuary away from the daily roughness of life. And the police were the last people she wanted to sabotage it. And anyway, she could protect herself if she prepared. Hence the giant carving knife in her hand.

"OK. Well, I thought I'd check in. Do you have someone with you?"

"Er, yes. My friend Kerry Oakland is here." Another lie. Her best friend was stuck in a psychiatric hospital. Her cheeks flushed. Was she allowed to lie to the police? Probably not. But it's not like she was lying about a crime. So surely it didn't matter. Her personal business wasn't his to know.

"OK. Good. I'll be driving around near your flat this evening, but if you feel unsafe at any point, please call 999, OK?"

"Yes, of course."

He hung up, and she went back to staring at the door, ears strained. DI Swanson was a good guy, but even he didn't believe the actual Lunar Killer was coming after her. Because as far as the police were concerned, they'd locked him up. He wasn't coming after Simone. DI Swanson had a minor concern it might be a copycat, which was why he kept calling. But for the most part, he thought she'd be safe. Or so he said.

She blinked hard and rubbed her tired eyes. There had to be some Red Bull in the fridge somewhere. She stood to search, still staring at the door, and snuck around as if trying not to wake a sleeping infant. But once standing, she froze deathly still.

There were footsteps coming down the corridor – heavy thuds, just like that night in the alley. And getting closer by the second. She whizzed around, looking for the knife she'd left on the floor. She spotted it and lunged towards it. But in her haste, her boot kicked the weapon, and it skidded away under the small dining table. She cursed and dived underneath to grab it.

But the heavy thuds stopped.

She froze under the table and faced the door. Someone was on the other side. She could hear a rustling of some sort.

Was it him?

Was he reaching for his own knife?

She stayed crouched on the floor. Her phone still in her shaking hand, she tried to scroll through her phone book to dial DI Swanson. He was of more use than ten of the other officers combined.

But her fingers were slow and shaky and wouldn't work. She shouldn't have been so damn stubborn. The rustling stopped and her head snapped back up to the door. The letterbox opened, and she cursed inwardly. She should have secured it.

For a moment, her entire world stood still. He'd trapped her, just as he did in the alley. He pushed something white through the letterbox.

She stared at the item. Was it a piece of paper? A note from her would-be killer? She didn't dare breathe and drew her eyes back up to the handle. But no other movement came from behind the door.

She held her breath. The ticking clock made the otherwise silent space even more intense and her heartbeat pounded in her head, begging her to take in some air. But seconds later, the heavy footsteps thudded away from the door and she could breathe again.

She stood, holding onto the kitchen counter for support. She stopped and listened, but no noise came from the corridor. The white item called for her attention and she tiptoed over to it. It was a piece of paper. An advert? She bent down to grab it and stepped quickly away from the door before turning it over.

It was junk mail. Some advertisements for local services. She'd nearly had a heart attack because of bloody junk mail.

Her cheeks burned. She was not a weak person. That bastard had made her this way, and he needed to pay. She threw the leaflet onto the kitchen table and brought her first down on top of it, but one advertisement on the leaflet caught her eye.

'Not feeling like yourself? Call me today.'

She grabbed the leaflet and stared at the words as if they made no sense. She unfolded it and a smiling picture of a man stared out at her. He had friendly eyes that were wrinkling with age, and a giant smile.

Theo Beckly. Licensed professional therapist. No wait list.

Surely it wasn't a coincidence. It was a sign. That's what normal people did when they were struggling, right? See a doctor. But she didn't need her own useless doctor who didn't listen to a word she said.

This therapist might be just what she needed to get rid of her anger. She took the leaflet back to her corner, knife in hand, and read through the details, making a mental note to call him first thing in the morning.

Theo

Theo Beckly shifted his weight in the doughy armchair and pulled down the sleeves of his white shirt so they covered his wrists in full. He twiddled the thick silver band on his right forefinger. The Christmas period always brought him new patients. The big day was two weeks away, and there were always people desperate for help to get through the pressures of the holiday period. New patients gave him a sort of excited, nervous energy. There was so much to learn about each other and so many ways the conversations could flow.

But mental illness was unpredictable. It took time to develop trust. Sometimes the conversation didn't go as well as he hoped and ended badly. And that part that made him nervous.

He glanced inside the thin folder on his knee. There wasn't much in there yet, just one page of the most basic details. His newest patient was Simone Johnson. A thirty-three-year-old journalist who lived on the other side of Derby City, not a million miles away from his own flat. A man attacked her six weeks ago and she wanted to talk through some of her anxiety since. It all sounded fairly standard. No health conditions or previous mental health diagnoses, so she said.

There was a soft knock at the door, and he looked up

expectantly. The door half opened and eighteen-year-old Tia popped her timid head around the frame, which surprised him. In her six weeks of working for him, Tia had never opened the door until he called out. Hopefully, that meant her confidence was growing.

"Simone Johnson's here for her appointment, Sir," she said politely. As usual, he tried not to laugh at her use of the word *Sir*. She was meticulously polite at all times and worked out to be a great fit for the clients so far. It was harder for people to get stressed or angry when faced with such a beautiful and polite young girl. Which was why he'd hired her. She had a calming effect on people.

"OK, let her in," he replied, reaching over to the desk behind him to put down the file. He would need to add her notes to the computer shortly, though he preferred the paper files he kept stored in a locked drawer.

Seconds later, a petite woman walked in. She'd tied her dark hair up in a tight bun and dressed more like a lawyer than a journalist with a white blouse tucked into a tight black skirt that grazed her knees. Dark glasses added to the lawyer look. She stayed in the doorway and eyed him carefully as he stood. It was obvious he'd have to work hard to earn this one's trust.

"Hi, Simone," he gave her the biggest smile he could muster without appearing a creep. "I'm Theo Beckly. Please take a seat."

"Hi, Theo," she replied in a soft voice. She followed his hand to take a seat on the flowery couch opposite his chair.

He waited until she'd sat down before returning to his own seat. She carefully placed her handbag on the floor in front of her and fixed her stare back at him. Some patients liked to control the room from the second they walked in and would start the conversation straight away. But Simone Johnson didn't say a word.

"How are you today, Simone?" he asked.

"I'm good, thank you," she replied.

She had a fierce look in her eyes. It gave her presence despite her small stature, but it wasn't confidence in her eyes. Mistrust, maybe. That wouldn't be unusual.

"Great!" Theo kept his voice level, but friendly. "Have you ever had therapy before?"

She shook her head. His eyes flicked down to her lap. She balled her palms into tight fists and rested them on her thigh.

"OK. How about we start off with me telling you how it works?"

She nodded. She wasn't making his job easy with so few words.

"So, I specialise in Cognitive Behavioural Therapy – or CBT for short. It's a talking therapy, and we'll look at your negative thought patterns around certain activities and aim to improve them by making your thoughts in that situation more positive."

He paused to gauge her reaction. She still stared at him. Had she even blinked since she walked in?

"You make it sound so easy," she said, and the corners of her mouth upturned the tiniest bit.

Was that almost a smile?

"Nothing worth it is ever easy," he replied with his own smile to encourage her to relax. *You definitely won't be easy.*

"That's true, I suppose." She shrugged as if indifferent.

She tore her stare away from him and peered above his head instead. She focused on the colourful artwork on the wall behind him. The art he'd placed there specially for people who didn't like to look him in the eye when revealing their secrets, which he suspected was Simone.

"OK. Your turn. Tell me what brought you here today?" he asked.

Her eyes shot back to him, and he couldn't stop himself from looking away and fidgeting in his seat. *Damn it.* There was something about her eyes that got to him. He forced his body to sit still and fixed a friendly stare straight back at her.

"I was attacked six weeks ago by a man. A stranger. He tried to kill me." She kept her eyes on his easily, rather than peering back at the artwork. He'd been wrong. That didn't happen often. "But he failed thanks to some voices nearby. They scared him away."

"Sorry to hear that. That must have been tough."

She nodded once more. This was going to be a long session. But a challenge was always a good thing. And his intrigue grew by the second. Nothing about Simone matched. Her clothes didn't suit her quiet personality. Her nervous personality didn't suit the way she stared at him and spoke easily. She was a puzzle that needed to be figured out.

"So, what specifically brings you here to see me?" He tried again.

She sighed and clasped her hands together on her lap.

"I guess I want to know why. I want to know what makes a man feel so weak he attempts to murder an innocent woman on the street."

She said the words with little emotion, though she was clearly upset. Who wouldn't be after such an ordeal? He needed to reach that feeling somehow. Maybe a blunter approach would work. "Maybe to him you weren't innocent?" he suggested.

"What do you mean?" she snapped, her pale cheeks glowing a rosier colour.

He smiled. There was the emotion he wanted to reach.

"You think you're innocent, but maybe he thinks you are not. It could have been mistaken identity, for example."

She opened her mouth as if to argue, but paused and looked away once more.

"You might never know why he did it, Simone. And it could be as simple as it was dark. He was drunk, and he thought you were his evil ex-girlfriend. But the answer to that question shouldn't rule your life. *He* shouldn't rule your life."

He watched her face soften as his suggestion sunk in. Maybe he could reach her after all. He could feel a connection already. And he wanted to know all about Simone Johnson. She was special. A tough nut to crack for sure. But he already knew she'd be worth it.

Simone

Six weeks later, Simone eyed Theo Beckly carefully through her thick glasses. There was a smudge on the left lens, which made his right eye look strangely distorted. She ignored the smudge, liking the way it made him appear imperfect. As if she wasn't the only one in the room with problems.

"Simone Johnson, glad to see you back," Theo said in his familiar, smooth tone. His therapist's voice. He spoke differently to the young receptionist. More relaxed. He'd told Simone he'd lived in Derby all his life, but his accent was more polished than the usual east midlands accent. Maybe he faked it, like she had when working in customer service through university.

"Glad to see you, too," she replied, meaning every word. Her life had improved tenfold since starting therapy, and a month and a half into their sessions, she was very glad she'd met Theo Beckly. She watched him shift position in his grey armchair. It was the same type of chair that she'd seen therapists use in films. The entire room looked just as you'd expect in a film, complete with certifications on the walls.

He was always shifting in his chair, as though she made him uncomfortable somehow. She pondered if he knew more about her than he let on. He looked at her as if he *knew* something was off.

"Where shall we start today?" he asked.

She didn't answer straight away. He smiled at her, showing off his perfectly straight teeth. She knew what she wanted to tell him, and butterflies fluttered in her stomach. Or maybe it was just nerves. Or it could be the smell of the nearby city centre takeaways, seeing as his office was located close to a string of kebab houses and pizza palaces. At least his rates were low, though.

"Where would you suggest we start?" she asked.

"Well, we could continue to talk about the death of your aunt?" he suggested. He fiddled with the ring on his right hand. He was always messing with that damn ring. "She died when you were twenty-two, correct? Eleven years ago."

"Yes. She died of cancer six years after I went to live with her," Simone answered automatically. She noticed he no longer looked distorted since he'd shifted in his chair, and took off her glasses to wipe the smudge away.

"Six years after your mother died?"

Simone looked away from his intense stare. "Yes, but I'd rather not talk about that."

"OK. What would you like to talk about?"

She turned her gaze back to him and replaced her glasses. "Well, I have a confession."

She watched him carefully, but he didn't react. Theo didn't look like a stereotypical therapist with his clean-cut black hair. He was the least therapist-like thing in the room. It had surprised her at how young he looked, maybe late thirties at most. He'd looked older in the advert that someone posted through her door. She would never have sought therapy if it hadn't been for that advert. It was as if someone knew what she needed. Maybe it was her dad watching over her.

Theo uncrossed his legs and leaned forward in his chair. "OK. Shoot," he replied.

She took a breath to make sure her voice stayed level. "I think I deserved what happened to me."

It was subtle, but she noted Theo's eyes widened and one eyebrow raised just a little. He was great at keeping his feelings hidden. Almost as good as her.

"No. You didn't deserve it," he said simply.

Simone leaned back. "How do you know? I must have done something to deserve it. And you don't know me that well, really."

He shook his head. "Nobody deserves to be brutally attacked from behind and almost killed in the street by someone twice their size."

She scoffed. "Some people do."

"No, Simone. They don't. I've worked with people who have done terrible things because of their upbringing, or because of their mental health. It doesn't make them evil. Everybody deserves to be safe and have a chance to be *good* despite their past."

She didn't respond, taken aback by his passion. In some ways, Theo was the best man she'd ever met. He was non-judgemental, kind and protective, and far more interesting than she'd expected him to be.

But he was wrong.

"If you say so." She shrugged.

He laughed. "I take it you don't agree?"

She pondered his words for a moment. "I think many people deserve a second chance, just not *everybody*."

"Everybody is a strong word, I agree." He was always smiling to the point she couldn't imagine him ever losing his temper. But his job called for a lot of patience, she supposed.

In fact, despite her vulnerability, talking to Theo was the most open and honest she'd been with a man since Dad died, and that was almost twenty years ago. She thought for a moment. It was eighteen years, to be exact. Seventeen years since Mum died. She'd been on her own so long she'd almost forgotten what it was like to have someone to talk to. Yes, meeting Theo Beckly was definitely one of her better decisions. But then, her decisions always had a way of going wrong.

One hour later, Simone was back in her flat and frying some chicken to add to a shop-bought jar of jalfrezi sauce. Before the attack, she loved to cook from scratch. She'd search the aisles of the local farm shop for the perfect ingredients, inhaling the smell of the fresh produce. It was calming to focus on blending tastes and textures together to create something special, even if it was only for her to taste since Kerry went to the hospital.

But she hadn't visited the farm shop since that night in the alley. Making fancy meals from scratch was suddenly so pointless when she was alone. It's not like anyone else was around to see the result. So, she'd make enough curry so she wouldn't have to cook again for two nights.

She threw in the jar of sauce and flicked on the TV whilst she waited for the chicken to cook in the bland flavours of the jar. The living room and kitchen were one open space, with a bedroom and bathroom off the two doors behind the sofa. She sat on the small sofa and kept the volume on the TV low enough so she could hear any noise from beyond the front door.

The problem with living in a block of flats was that there was always noise coming and going. She could hear footsteps most of the day or night. But she always kept the volume low to listen for the heavy thud of his boots.

Theo recommended moving, but that was impossible on her wage. She'd have to stump up the deposit somehow, plus agent fees for pushing some paperwork around. She needed a minimum of two thousand pounds, probably closer to three. And that would not be forthcoming anytime soon. Especially not on the paltry sick pay given by the local rag.

She flicked to the true crime channel. One obsession she was not ready to give up was her documentaries, despite Theo's request. He didn't think it was good for her anxiety. But he didn't realise that it helped to watch the process of a killer being caught, as did seeing survivors living their best life. Some people had suffered much worse than a few kicks. She was lucky in a way.

It was also fascinating to see *why* the killer hurt people. What was their excuse, if any? The channel was halfway through a documentary about Ted Bundy, but she'd seen his story so many times that she settled into it easily.

Until she heard the heavy thud of boots outside her front door.

She grabbed the remote and flicked off the TV, perched on the edge of the sofa. She listened to the footsteps. The curry sizzled quietly, but she didn't move to turn it off.

The footsteps stopped right outside her door, but only for a second before continuing down the hallway. She breathed and tiptoed over to the curry to turn off the sizzling pan. Anger filled her. This pathetically scared version of her had to go.

She was going after him.

She grabbed the knife that she'd used to chop chicken. May as well give the bastard salmonella if he was outside. She snuck over to the front door and listened again. The corridor was silent now. She grasped the handle and prised the door open, thrusting her head into the corridor and searching in both directions.

But no one was there.

She lowered her shaking hand. Maybe she was going crazy and would end up sharing a room with Kerry. She slammed the flat door closed, her heart still beating a million miles an hour. She looked around the empty flat and pulled out her phone. Her finger hovered over DI Swanson's name, but really, what could he do? He didn't really care about her. He was just a police officer doing his job.

She scrolled back up to Theo Beckly's number and hit dial before she had time to talk herself out of it. Though she almost hung up when he answered straight away.

"Simone? Are you OK?" His concerned voice calmed her immediately.

"Yes, I'm OK. I just wondered if I left my glasses at your office?" She flung open her door again and glanced one more time down the corridor. Nothing.

"Oh. Erm, give me a sec." She heard a rustling noise as if he was searching his paper covered desk. "I don't think so. Sorry."

"That's OK." She paused, wishing she could think of something else to say.

"Are you sure you're OK?" he asked again.

"Yes. Of course. I'm surprised you're still working." She closed the flat door and made sure it was locked.

"I'm not. You were my last client of the day."

"Oh, I'm sorry. I just assumed because it seemed like you

22

were searching the office for my glasses? I shouldn't be bothering you at this time, anyway."

"It's fine. I really don't mind—"

"No, no. It's not OK, I'm sorry." She cut him off and hung up before he responded. But even a brief conversation with him made her feel less alone. And rather than thinking about those heavy footsteps, she suddenly looked forward to the next time she saw Theo Beckly.

Theo

Theo sipped on a tall glass of water to settle his nervous stomach. Though something stronger would have worked better. Simone would appear through the door any minute, and he had a different aim to today's session. An unusual request to ask of a client. It was a colossal risk. Maybe their therapy would end altogether today.

The rays of the sun shone through the small window behind him and fingered the couch where Simone usually sat. It seemed fitting that it would light her up today, of all days. The same day he wanted to find out if she felt the same connection he did.

Tia pushed open the door, not even bothering to knock now. She nodded to him, and he smiled back to confirm he was ready for his client. He reached to the desk behind him to put the glass of water on a coaster and put a hand to his stomach to settle the gurgling nerves.

Simone walked in as he turned back. But she looked different today. She wore little makeup usually, but today she wore none. Her hair was down and dishevelled, and didn't have the same sheen it usually held. Her glasses perched on the end of her nose. She smiled sheepishly and walked to the couch with her head down.

"What's wrong?" he asked before she'd even taken a seat.

She just about sat down before taking one look at him and bursting into tears. Her hands flew up to cover her face. He stood and rushed to his desk for the box of tissues, practically throwing them at her once he'd found them. He stood awkwardly in front of her. Usually, he would sit as a client cried and would never offer them a hug. Professional boundaries, and all that jazz. But with Simone it took every fibre in his being not to reach out to her and give her some comfort. He forced himself back down in his armchair as she sobbed into a tissue.

"OK, Simone. Breathe. Do you want some water?"

She breathed in sharply and removed the tissue from her face. She shook her head and dried her eyes. The odd sob still escaped, but she was far more under control. Thank God. It was horrible to see her so upset.

"OK. Take your time and then tell me what's wrong."

"Oh, it's so stupid." She shook her head as if ashamed of herself.

"I'll be the judge of that." He smiled.

She smiled back, but said nothing and continued to dab her eyes, though they were already drying. Hmm. She rarely stalled. He'd not met many people as bravely honest as Simone. She usually blurted out whatever was on her mind. But she clearly needed some serious cheering up today.

"Did the shop run out of Krispy Kremes or something?" he asked. Her smile grew wider, but it was very subtle. "Did you get too drunk and fall over with your pants down?"

Her face dropped immediately, as did his stomach.

"What's wrong Simone? What did I say?"

She sighed so loud it almost echoed around the room. "I went out to have a drink. My boss, Jenny. She was insistent that it would help, even though I told her alcohol is a depressant." She waved a hand around, almost as if she was drunk now. "And then walking home, well, the night I was attacked, I was also out with Jenny and the team. The walk home was the same one."

Her eyes drifted away from him. She stopped talking, though her mouth was still open. He gave her a minute, not wanting to interrupt her thought flow.

"And then I don't really know what happened. Jenny said she'd walk me home. I thought I saw the man near my flat. I screamed and made a total show of myself. Jenny called the police, who thought I was crazy."

She stopped again but put her head in her hands as if she were about to cry again. That couldn't happen.

"Simone, that sounds completely normal to me," he spoke in his most reassuring tone.

"Theo, I can't even go for a drink. It's not like I go out often, but I want the choice to do it without going bloody crazy."

This was his chance. A natural lead to ask her for a drink. "Well, I have some homework for you," he said carefully. He needed to gauge her reaction and choose his words wisely. "Go out and try again. Have some fun. So what if you failed the first time? Try again."

She shook her head vehemently. "I can't! You weren't there. I made a holy show of myself."

"Is there anything else you like to do for fun?"

She fell silent and chewed on her bottom lip, deep in thought. "I like to read."

"What do you like to read?"

"Anything really. My favourite is a book Dad gave me." She

26

looked away wistfully with a small smile. "It's '*Little Women*'. Reading that usually calms me. But I want to be able to go outside, you know? I want the choice. I feel like that's been taken away from me."

"Well, what if we do some therapy together outside?"

She glanced at the window behind him. "Outside?" Her nose wrinkled in confusion.

"Yes, outside. We can have a drink – non-alcoholic, of course. And I can walk back with you and talk you through your thoughts. It would give you some strategies to help with the negative thought processes that make you panic."

At first, he could have sworn her face lit up at the suggestion, but it soon darkened. She stared at the floor for a moment.

"Sorry, I don't think I can do that." And with that, she stood up and stalked straight to the exit.

"Simone! Wait, please," Theo called, but she didn't even turn to look at him as she walked through the door.

He froze in the middle of the room, torn between running after her and sitting back down. He cursed. When Simone was around, he couldn't think straight. He racked his brain trying to imagine what he would do if a regular client walked out like that. And he knew the answer. He grabbed the glass of water and threw it at the wall. He watched the shards of glass splinter everywhere and sat back down in his armchair. Clearly, he was wrong. She didn't yet feel the same connection. And that would not do.

Simone

A few days later Simone sat at her desk, unable to focus on the boring story she was supposed to be writing about a new swimming bath opening near the city centre. She remembered going swimming with her dad every Saturday morning until secondary school. They'd splash about and the local pool would get a big inflatable park out to jump all over. They stopped that now though, thanks to health and safety gone mad. Who even went swimming these days? Unless it was in a pretty waterfall which looked good on Instagram, nobody cared.

The dull office didn't help her mood. She was glad it was pretty empty. Jill sat on the other side in her own world. As the oldest member of the team, she was near retirement, and did little work other than count down the days until she would leave. But most people were out for lunch. Simone hadn't bothered. She didn't want to eat. She'd meekly agreed to allow someone to bring her back a Subway sandwich, but her stomach flipped at the thought of having to eat it. Maybe she'd save it for dinner.

It was Friday. Which was the same day she usually had therapy with Theo. Except she wasn't going today. She'd run out on him the previous week because no matter how carefully he'd worded it, she'd almost said yes to a date with him. And that would not happen. Sure, a part of her wanted to get to know Theo better, but a date was the last thing she needed.

Returning to work had made for a rough week though. Everything still seemed so pointless. And she couldn't deny that Theo was the only thing she could think of.

"Simone, go home."

Jenny's voice came from nowhere, and Simone jerked around to see her boss right behind her. God knows how she'd sneaked up on her. The stench of her perfume alone usually gave her away a mile off.

"Home? Why?" Simone asked.

Jenny sighed. "Because you clearly aren't ready to be here, love."

She hated the sympathy in Jenny's eyes. It made her adamant to stay. But Jenny was right. She wasn't ready to be here. She couldn't think of anywhere she wanted to be *less* than here.

"Listen, I haven't done your return to work forms yet. Get another sick note for a week, and we'll pretend it's just one instance of sickness. Do something that cheers you up. Take your mind off things. Maybe see that aunt of yours."

Simone nodded, unsure if she was happy to be going home or pissed off at being on the receiving end of Jenny's sympathy. And momentarily thrown off that she'd forgotten Jenny thought her aunt was still alive. As far as Jenny knew, that's whom Simone spent Christmas day with; because no way would she be allowed to spend it alone as she desired. Jenny squeezed her shoulder and retreated to her private office.

Simone grabbed her bag and jacket and headed for the exit. She realised halfway across the car park she'd have no Subway sandwich for dinner. No matter, she'd have to stop at the shop to pick something up.

She turned left out of the car park to walk the long way home. The shop was on the way and she wouldn't have to walk through the godforsaken alley. The owners had put a light and a camera up now. Too little too late for Simone.

The streets were fairly busy as usual for a Friday lunchtime. Every pub she passed had people outside with a pint in one hand and a cigarette in the other. She breathed in the smoke as she passed, missing the days she used to be drunk with a cigarette in her hand, too young to care about consequences like cancer.

It only took a few minutes to reach the small shop, and she was glad to see most of the lunchtime rush had ended as people made their way back to various offices. It didn't have loads of choice, but there was a small section of frozen, microwaveable dinners for pathetic people like her.

She walked straight to the end of the row to the frozen aisle and browsed the woeful offerings. It was fortunate she didn't want a large meal, as the servings were always so tiny in microwave meals. Especially the diet ones. She raised her gaze to browse through some meals in the top freezer, but the reflection she saw made her own blood flow like ice.

The man with piercing blue eyes was right behind her.

Theo

As soon as she screamed, Theo knew it was Simone. He ran down the aisle toward the harrowing noise. And there she was, standing in front of the freezer section. Her hand clutched her chest, her face whiter than he'd ever seen it. He rushed in her direction, stopping about a foot away.

"Hey! Simone!" he called out to her above the screams. "What is it? What's wrong?"

"He's here!" she shrieked, pointing down the aisle. "He's found me!"

"Where?" Theo turned to stare in the direction she pointed, but there was nobody there other than an old lady looking thoroughly confused.

An overweight man nearing retirement jogged over, his face red and sweaty. He wore the orange and blue colours of the store on his shirt.

"What's going on?" he demanded, his face contorted in rage.

Simone burst into tears. Theo glanced at the sweaty man's name tag. The plain black letters confirmed his name was 'Jerry,' and he was the store manager. Great. A jacked-up middle management idiot.

"Nothing, Sir. We're just leaving," Theo responded and put his hand on the small of Simone's back to steer her away from the foaming Jerry. She let him guide her easily, in too much of a panic to disagree. Her body heaved with heavy sobs and her breathing came in erratic waves.

"It's OK, Simone. Whoever it was has gone now." He kept his voice as calm as possible as he steered her through nosy onlookers.

Once outside, Simone leant against the wall and crouched down with her head between her knees. It hurt her sore thigh to bend down, but she didn't care. Her body shook with tears and she removed her glasses and held her face in her hands. Theo fished a packet of tissues out of his coat pocket and knelt down beside her, forcing the packet into her hand.

"Here, take one of these."

Her fingers squeezed around the tissues, and to his surprise, she laughed.

"Simone? Are you laughing?" he asked, bewildered.

She laughed even harder at that, her sobs gradually turning into raucous giggles. He couldn't help but laugh with her.

"What on earth are you laughing at?"

She lifted her head. Her face was blotchy with tears, but she grinned. "I've just never known a man to carry little packets of tissues."

He snorted with laughter. "Are you taking the piss out of me right now? You're the one who's just been screaming in the freezer section of a shop!"

She burst into uncontrollable laughter and fell to the floor laughing. When she stopped, her face was bright red, and she was out of breath. She put her hand out to him, and he grabbed it to help her up off the floor.

She wiped her face with one final tissue and replaced her glasses. "Jesus. I've actually gone crazy, haven't I?"

"I think maybe you needed a giggle." He smiled.

"You're always smiling. Are you this jolly outside of work?"

"You could always find out."

Regret punched him in the stomach. Talking to her outside of his office was making him act out of therapist mode. Why the hell had he said that? He took a step back and waited for the backlash.

"Maybe I will," she said with a sly smile. "I have to go, but thanks for getting me out of there. I'll call you."

Forget hiding his emotions, his eyes almost popped out of his head. Had Simone Johnson just agreed to a date? He swallowed an urge to ask if he could walk her home. The last thing he needed was to tempt fate after she'd finally admitted there was a connection between them.

But he watched her walk away with a grin on his face. He knew she felt it, too. All he had to do now, was convince her to move in with him.

Simone

S imone stared at Theo for the first time since the shop incident, and though she hadn't called him like she'd promised, she knew she'd made the right decision to return to him. Seeing him kept her sane. And truth be told, she wanted him to ask her for another drink. The last time she'd felt that way about a guy was a very long time ago, and that hadn't ended well.

"Hi, Simone, great to see you again." He gave her one of his regular smiles, and her stomach fluttered.

"Good to see you, too," she replied and smiled back.

"So, how have you been?" he asked.

She shrugged and pulled her eyes away from him to stare at the only artwork in the room, which happened to be a colourful piece above his head. There wasn't much else to look at on the plain, white walls, save a precariously stacked bookcase and a green plant which was taller than her. Though it wasn't difficult to be taller than her. Maybe it was supposed to be calming. She'd read an article once on the relaxation powers of plants. Maybe that's what she needed in her flat. More plants.

"I'm OK, thanks, really sorry that I missed the last session. I was confused about how I wanted to proceed. Therapy wise, of course."

She tucked a piece of stray hair behind her ear and gave him a shy smile in return. Inwardly, she cursed herself for not getting her hair done before seeing him. The split ends fell well past her shoulders now, and she could have done with the confidence boost that came with fresh hair.

"That's OK." He nodded and looked at her expectantly. Was he hoping for an explanation about the shop? He'd be waiting a while. She didn't want to discuss that any further than they already had. "Well, the last time we spoke, officially, you might remember that I gave you some homework?"

"Yes. I remember your homework. You told me to have some fun." Her smile faltered. "I tried, but I didn't really manage it, I'm afraid to say."

"So, you didn't do the homework, and you missed the last session prior to getting upset in the shop. Do you want to talk about either of those things?" There was no annoyance in his voice, only concern. He leant further forward and clasped his hands together across his knees.

Simone leant forward too, mirroring his body language, the warm feeling she got when he paid attention to her returning. She'd almost forgotten how he made her confidence grow. He clearly cared for her wellbeing. He'd made that clear in the previous session. She should have gone for it then. It would have been less awkward with him making the first move.

"Well, yes. OK. I know I hurried out of here last time when you were trying to be ... friendly." She paused to gauge his reaction, but his face appeared frozen. He didn't even blink, though his cheeks coloured slightly. "And so firstly I wanted to apologise for that. I shouldn't have reacted that way."

Theo cleared his throat. "If I was overly friendly last time, Simone, I'm truly, *truly* sorry. I really feel like we have such

35

a great connection, and I thought I might be able to help you relax in the social situations you've come to dread since the attack. That's really all I meant by going for a drink."

Simone nodded and allowed her eyes to drift to the floor, not really knowing how to say what she had come to talk about. She always struggled to get her words straight around Theo, and not because of his striking eyes or the muscles that could be seen pushing against his thin shirt. He was so calm. And so confident. The two things she'd always wished she could be.

"Simone, I see what I said was stupid now. It was completely unprofessional of me, and I'm sorry from the bottom of my heart. I hope you can forgive me." He sounded so sincere, but then Theo always did.

"It's OK. I wasn't mad at you or upset by what you said," Simone answered. She shivered, despite the warmth of the office, and pulled her denim jacket tighter around her and crossed her arms together.

"You *weren't* mad at me?" He leant back in his chair, his face expressionless. He was good at that. It must be a requirement of the job. She briefly wondered what types of fears and confessions he heard about inside these walls. Probably just as bad as what she heard writing for the local rag. Many people who rang the paper with their ridiculous stories could do with therapy.

She shook her head and pushed away the thoughts so she could focus on what she came to say. "It was just a bit unexpected, and I was scared then. But I'm ready now. I've had time to think it over and to process what you said. Especially since you helped me in the shop. The truth is, Theo, this is the only time I have fun. This is the only place I feel safe enough to laugh and let go." The words came easier than she expected.

"This?" he tilted his head to one side like an eager puppy.

"Yes. This. Here. When I'm with you." Simone stood up and hoped he couldn't see her trembling legs.

Theo put up a hand as if to stop her. "Simone, I have to tread carefully here. Please don't think I'm pushing you away, but as a therapist it's unethical of me to—" But he stopped talking as Simone reached him and his hand fell. He looked at the door and back to Simone, mouth still hanging open.

"But I'm not crazy, Theo. I'm not one of your vulnerable patients. It's OK to want me. I want you, too." She reached her hand out, hoping it wasn't too sweaty, and he gripped it tightly.

Without a word, he allowed her to pull him up from the armchair, and suddenly he was looking down at her. Damn, if only she'd worn heels. This wouldn't be so awkward.

"I just have one more thing to tell you," she whispered as she stared up at him.

"Yes?" he struggled to utter the word.

"I quit your therapy sessions. Sorry, they just weren't working out."

As soon as she'd said the words, Theo wrapped his arms around her and leant down to meet her lips, kissing her hard. A wave of relief washed over Simone. He was finally all hers, and he was what she needed to keep safe.

Theo

Six glorious weeks passed since he had first kissed Simone, and Theo still couldn't believe his amazing luck to be close to her. Those weeks had been full of romantic Peak District walks, top-notch restaurants and one cinema trip. The film was terrible, but that didn't matter as long as they were together.

He'd even caved and gone ice skating in Nottingham Ice Arena, which was about as far away from his usual hobbies as he could get. Simone barely let go of the training penguin, despite begging him to go. She said it was a childhood dream, but her mother disapproved and her dad had died before he got the chance to take her. Though he'd been reluctant, he'd never laughed so much on a date.

And now he was in Simone's kitchen and perched at the smallest dining table he'd ever seen. It was only made for two, so the chairs slotted under the table to save space. It certainly wasn't of any use to anyone over five and a half feet tall. The flat she rented was in Normanton, just on the outskirts of Derby city centre. It wasn't too far from his own shared flat, maybe a ten-minute walk. Though his place was much bigger.

She sat across from him, and he stared into her dark eyes. He could get lost in them for hours if that wouldn't make him look like a complete weirdo.

"So, I had a thought about this place," he said, choosing his words carefully. "You're super unhappy here, lots of terrible memories, yes?"

She nodded and raised an eyebrow. "I'm not moving in with you yet, if that's what you're going to suggest!"

He threw his head back and laughed at her suggestion. "You'll have to work harder to get into my flat!" he teased. She slapped his hand, and he grabbed hers and squeezed it tight.

"But why don't we look at fresh places for you to live? Why stay here?"

"I can't afford to move! I'm too busy paying rent to save up for a deposit, and I don't want your money before you suggest it."

"You don't need to. How about I just get you somewhere to stay for a month, and you can save your rent money and bills and choose somewhere new to live?"

She shook her head. "I don't want your money, Theo!"

"I'm not giving you money, so don't think of it like that. I'm just giving you some time. That way you get out of this flat straight away, no messing around. No more being terrified of that damn alley. You can get signed off from work for a month. I'll write a note for your doctor. Just relax, feel better and look forward to a new life."

She chewed on her bottom lip, a sign she was deep in thought. He dared to hope she would say yes. A break would do her a world of good. He gave her a few more moments to think over his suggestion and peered around the kitchen walls. She'd filled them with various photos, clocks and calendars. She'd decorated it nicely for a shoe-string budget like hers – and it pleased him to see there was none of that slogan rubbish he hated. *'Live, Laugh, Love'* in the entry hall, or 'SOAK' right above the bath, as if people didn't know what a bloody bath was for. He didn't want that in their eventual shared home.

"So, what do you think?" he asked as he turned back to her. He leant back on the chair casually, trying not to let his nerves show.

She turned her head to meet his gaze. "Well, I love the idea of it, babe. Really, I do." She looked down at the ground with a defeatist expression. He hated seeing that look in her eyes. It was a look of pain. It didn't show very often, but it broke him when it did.

"Let me help you. That's what I'm here for, aren't I?" Her fingers were so soft as he wrapped his hand even tighter around hers.

"We're here for *each other*, but I don't want to accept your money yet. We haven't known each other long. I don't want anyone thinking I'm after your money!"

She squeezed his hand back, and he fought an urge to stand and take her to the bedroom.

"Who would you worry about thinking that? Nobody would even know." Maybe they didn't need to go to the bedroom. He could just reach across right now and kiss her ears in that tickly way she liked.

"*I'd* know." She looked at him with a determined pout that made her even sexier.

He couldn't control himself any longer and was on his feet before he realised what he was doing. He put his arms around her and breathed in her sweet scent. Simone always smelled of pink grapefruit body wash. She had two showers a day without fail. It was yet another thing he loved about her. *Cleanliness is next to Godliness* was his favourite childhood adage. He stared at her for a moment. She could have anyone, and she'd chosen him.

"OK. Just let me know if you change your mind," he said as he bent down to kiss her cheek.

She turned to him, reaching his lips with hers. He kissed her gently and teased her with his tongue before running a hand through her hair and kissing her neck. His hand slipped up her top to reach for her breast. She allowed it for a few seconds before she pushed his hand away.

Simone always liked to be in control. That was fine with him. It made a pleasant change from the usual women he dated.

"Come on." She grabbed his hand, and he allowed her to guide him to the living room, willing her to walk quicker.

She pushed him down onto the sofa and stood in front of him. He watched as she carefully removed her pink satin blouse and black pencil skirt. She left her black heels on, watching his expression the whole time. He ran his eyes over her body, taking in the curve of her hip and the small rolls on her stomach that made him want her even more.

He loved her imperfections more so than any other part of her body, like the angry, red slash on her right thigh. Only he got to see these areas. They were special. They were *his*. She removed her bra and stepped closer to him so he could reach out and touch her silky skin, running his hand up along her stomach and cupping her breasts. She moaned quietly.

"Please, Simone. Let me do what I need to do to make you feel safe. End your lease here. Let me rent somewhere for one month, and you can use that month's wage for a deposit on a new place. Please." He kissed her stomach, running his tongue down past her belly button but pulling back. "Please."

"OK," she breathed. "Now kiss me lower."

He grinned and pulled down her underwear to kiss the most private parts of her body. She was finally going to allow him to take care of her, and the first task to do so was getting her out of the damn city and away from those idiots she worked with. Nothing would make him happier than being the one person she trusted to look after her.

Simone

The following morning, Simone handed in her thirty-day notice to the landlord of the flat. She'd never been so relieved to move house. The flat had too many terrible memories. Every time she sat on the sofa, it reminded her of being in pain and trying to deal with what happened alone. But she wasn't alone anymore.

Over the next month, she packed up her meagre belongings and Theo organised a small local storage unit with a friend and dropped her stuff off for her, so they could fit more things per trip in by using the front seat. She packed three suitcases to bring with her. They were full of clothes, shoes, books and bathroom products, and she was feeling well prepared for a month's break in the Peak District cottage Theo found online.

There were two items she couldn't bear to touch until the last day of the move. Bertie Bear was one, and he sat next to her on the bed. Her mother's silver trinket box was the other. Well, the trinket box was originally her great-grandmother's. As Theo disappeared to lug her suitcases to his car, she reached under the empty bed frame to pull it out from its hiding spot. She sat on the frame and ran her fingers over the delicate flower pattern. As a child, she loved looking at the trinket box. Mum kept it on display in the middle shelf of a glass cabinet in the living room. She never allowed Simone to touch it as a child. One of the first things Simone did after her mother died was hide the trinket box in her own belongings so nobody would take it away.

"What's that you've got, babe?" Theo's voice made her recoil so much she almost threw the damn trinket box at him.

"Jeez, don't sneak up on me like that!" She tried to catch the breath that had gotten stuck in her throat.

"Sorry!" Theo replied, though he was grinning. He held his hands up. "I didn't mean to, I swear. What are you hiding behind your back?"

Simone eyed him up and down, still annoyed at being scared. His face dropped as he realised she wasn't joking around.

"Oh, is it something private? I'm sorry. Do you want me to go?" He turned away awkwardly in the doorway. "I'll go. Sorry, babe. I'll just go."

Simone laughed quietly, and he spun around. "You don't have to go. It's OK. Here." She revealed the trinket box that was behind her back. "I didn't mean to hide it from you, but the meaning of it is difficult to talk about. It was my mother's."

Theo looked at her with sadness in his eyes. "It's beautiful. Just like you. And no doubt just like your mother was."

Simone nodded. "She was beautiful to look at."

Theo stepped over and sat down on the bed frame. "You never told me how your parents died."

She took a deep breath and looked up at him. He could handle the truth. There was no need to worry about that with Theo. She may as well spit out quickly. like ripping off a band aid.

"My dad was murdered. A year later, Mum killed herself with pills."

44

"Oh babe, that's horrendous. I'm so sorry. I shouldn't have asked. Do you want to talk about it?"

She shook her head and bent down to place the trinket on the floor. She turned to him with a playful grin.

"Who's this?" he asked, picking up Bertie Bear.

She took it from him and stroked the ear fondly. "Bertie Bear. My dad bought him for me the day he died. He'd been away for the night with work. He always brought me something back when he went away."

She placed Bertie Bear on the floor next to the trinket box and slid into Theo's arms, resting her head on his shoulder. He kissed the top of her head and put his arms around her. She stroked his chest, trailing her fingers down his stomach.

"I do think we should have one final bit of fun before leaving this place. Make my last memory a good one," she murmured, leaning up to kiss his neck.

"Anything you say." Theo grinned back as she pushed him down and climbed on top of him.

Two days later, the heavy front door to the cottage creaked as Simone closed it behind her. She yanked the handle hard to double-check it had locked shut. Once satisfied it was secure, she stepped over to the small closet to the left of the entry hall and removed her white trainers and denim jacket. It felt good to take off her trainers after a long walk around the Peak District hills. She stood still to take in the silence and took a deep breath. A slow smile spread across her face. She was home.

Well, it was home for now.

The relaxing scent of patchouli and sandalwood greeted her as it drifted through from the living room reed diffuser she'd purchased the day before. One of her favourite scents. She pulled on a pair of faux-fur slippers and walked through the narrow corridor to the living room.

The little stone cottage was hers for a whole month as Theo had promised. In two days, it already felt one hundred times more comfortable than her previous flat. That had always been poky and depressing, but it turned completely claustrophobic after the man attacked her right outside.

She sunk into the high-backed sofa and took another deep breath of the woody aroma. It had taken two days to unpack and a wave of tiredness took over. She took a moment to sit and appreciate the living room. It certainly wasn't how she'd decorate if she owned such a cute cottage, but she couldn't deny the rustic interior suited the isolated location of the house. Even if it was distasteful. Two dim wall lights were attached to a pair of antlers jutting out from the left-hand wall, and the sofa cushions were emblazoned with the image of a deer.

It was in a peaceful, wooded area of the Peak District with no neighbours for at least a mile. The nearest place to civilization was the picturesque village of Edale, three miles away. Which marked the start of the beautiful Pennine Way trail, stretching 268 long miles across the countryside. Or maybe it marked the end of the trail, depending on how you looked at it.

She stretched out on the sofa, enjoying the silence. The city was never silent. At the very least cars would drive by every few minutes all night long, putting her on edge wondering if her attacker was coming back to finish her just like the Lunar Killer did to his victims. A shiver ran down her spine at the thought of him. But that was stupid. The police had locked him away, probably somewhere far away. He had been for a couple of years. And as long as he was locked away, Simone could enjoy the peace of no one knowing where she lived.

Her phone's ringtone swiftly ruined that peace. She tugged it out of her jeans pocket, almost not wanting to look in case it was Jenny. Though she'd agreed to another month off, there was little chance of her not calling at all to check in. Simone's smile grew wider, however, when Theo's name flashed up.

"Hey, babe," she said warmly.

"Hi, are you OK?" he replied. He sounded rushed.

Simone sat up on the sofa, perching on the edge. "Sure, why wouldn't I be?" she asked.

"Oh, you know. Just wanted to see how you were settling in. I wanted to come and see you, but I've got a bit of an emergency with a patient." He sounded out of breath.

"Is that why you sound so strange?" she asked.

"Probably. Sorry, babe. A lady got a bit distressed and tried to attack me, but I'm fine. You remember Tia, my assistant? She helped to calm them until an ambulance arrived. The patient is safe now. Are you sure you're OK on your own?"

It was just like Theo to worry about her, even after someone had just attacked *him*. Simone sank back into the soft cushions. She definitely wanted some of these for her new place. Maybe not with deer on them, though.

"I'm OK as long as you're sure you are OK?"

"I'm fine, honestly!" he said with a laugh. He'd caught his breath and sounded much more normal.

"I'm better than OK, to be honest, babe. I can't thank you enough for putting me up here. It's so peaceful, and so generous of you. And hearing your voice always makes me feel better."

"I bet you can think of some ways to make it up to me," he said in a much lighter tone.

Simone laughed. "Yes. I might think of one or two special

ways to make it up to you if you can find time to come and see me soon?"

"Yes, of course! I'll be around tomorrow, is that OK? It's Friday, so I can sleep over with you and won't have to worry about work on Saturday."

"Sounds perfect. I'll make you a homemade beef and ale pie." Simone said, briefly wondering how she would get to the shop without his car. It didn't matter; she'd make it somehow. The thought of cooking from scratch again excited her. "You do like pie, right?"

"I love anything you make for me, but especially homemade pie. Did I ever tell you how perfect you are? What did I do to deserve you?"

Simone felt her cheeks heat up. Thank god he hadn't video called. "It's me that doesn't deserve you. I have an amazing therapist, a best friend and a sexy boyfriend all wrapped up in one."

He laughed again. "Be careful or my head will be too big to fit through the door, and then I won't be able to come and visit or eat the pie."

"Oh, well, your cooking still sucks. Did that help to shrink it?" she joked.

"Yes, yes, it helped a lot. I'd better go, beautiful. Call me if you need anything at all, right? Even just for a chat if the peace gets too peaceful. Anything at all," he said.

"Yes, yes. I will. Stop worrying. I'm feeling much calmer out here. Honestly, it's helping loads." She hoped he could hear sincerity in her voice.

"Good, that's what I want to hear. Love you."

Her heart still jumped a mile at his words. He was the first man to say them since Dad died. She could still hear his voice every night at bedtime. *'Love you, baby girl, don't let the bedbugs bite.'*

"Love you, too," she replied.

She hung up and threw the phone next to her on the sofa. It bounced along the cushions and skidded to a halt at the end of the sofa. When it stopped, the silence did suddenly feel *too* peaceful. She stood and wandered into the hallway, not sure what to do with herself, and ended up in the kitchen.

She'd never seen so much wood in one room in her life. It was everywhere she looked. Which would have been OK if it all matched. Instead, the countertops were a deep shade of solid oak, whilst the dining table was a lighter pine colour. The floor was a red herringbone, whilst rustic timber beams straddled the white ceiling at intervals. The beams and flooring were beautiful, but the rest really was a bit too much for Simone's taste.

She grabbed a can of Diet Coke from the fridge and leant against the table to inspect the room. She needed inspiration for her new place when she found one. The countryside would be perfect. Somewhere not directly within a town and definitely no cities. So, the decor needed to fit that.

But it was peace she craved more than anything. And in the silence here, she'd found that. She needed a place where no one was around to be aware of her existence; unless she wanted them to be. This house should have been perfect. Except for the silhouette of a man standing right outside her back door.

Theo

Theo's head ached on the drive back home from where his patient hit him with her ridiculous pointy shoes. She'd accused him of wanting to touch her sexually during their session, ran into the reception and gone berserk to his PA before throwing her shoe at him. He couldn't wait for a beer to end the long-ass day with.

Five minutes later, he slammed the door of his Vauxhall Insignia shut and flicked the lock button with his nose, hands too full of shopping bags to lock it any other way. He rushed up the path to reach the entrance of an old, red-brick mill just off Barmley New Road in Derby City. Not that anyone had used it as an actual mill for years. It was now an apartment complex of one- and two-bedroomed flats, four storeys high.

Theo ran up the stone steps two at a time, passing by peeling paint and handwritten signs for lost cats and dodgy pyramid businesses. Out of habit, he paused briefly at the top of two flights of stairs to get his breath back, but there was no need. His fitness had improved quite a lot over the last few months. When he'd first moved in six months ago, his chest had almost burst after walking up the steps. Now he could run up and get his breath back in less than a few seconds.

The forced aerobic exercise was one unexpected benefit of

moving into the flat. Although lifting the small set of weights in the bedroom was actually fun, cardio sucked. He stood straight and put a hand on his chest. His heart wasn't beating fast at all.

He continued around the corner to flat number twenty-eight and fumbled for the key in the deep pocket of his double-breasted overcoat. After fighting with a piece of string, a thin wallet and a leaky bottle of hand sanitizer, the house keys eventually appeared and he unlocked the door. He cursed as a bang echoed through the silent flat when the door slammed shut behind him. That was going to annoy the old bat upstairs. No doubt she'd be down soon to complain.

"Richard?" he called out for his flatmate, who usually worked from home. But there was no response.

The handle of the plastic bags stretched as though it were about to break, and Theo rushed through the corridor and into the open-plan kitchen diner to throw the bags on the side before they split. Thankful they hadn't split on the stairs. That would have been embarrassing. He hung up his coat and went to grab a beer from the fridge, but a note on the kitchen counter stopped him in his tracks.

'Gone to mums for a week, phone died so couldn't text, Rich.'

Oh, great. If he'd have known Richard was going to be away, Simone could have stayed with him for a week. It sucked so much being so far away from her, unable to care for her after what she'd been through. She was better off in the woods where no one could get to her, but it didn't seem fair she had to be alone. Or, more specifically, that she had to be so far from *him*. He ripped the note from the fridge, crumpled it up into a ball and threw it into the bin.

There weren't loads of shopping in the bags; the cupboards

were already fairly full, so he'd mainly purchased fresh fruit and milk and other fridge items. It took only two minutes to stack it all away neatly in the relevant places. It was so much easier to find things when everything had its place and was in view. It had taken Richard some time to get used to it. He said it was ridiculous and laughed at first. But he saw the benefits eventually.

He grabbed a well-deserved beer and sat down on the lumpy old sofa, resting his head back. His first meeting with Simone came to mind. Her blue eyes cool against warmer skin. The attack was still fresh, and she was full of anxiety and fear. Though she had gotten stronger much quicker than he expected. Much quicker than most patients. According to her, it was all thanks to his therapy sessions followed by their out-of-hours rendezvous once she was no longer a client.

Spending the night with her again would be amazing. What was stopping him from being there right now? He looked at his watch; it was only 6:00 p.m. His emergency patient was now secure in hospital following her accusations, and his first appointment in the morning wasn't until 10:00 a.m. That was plenty of time to get back from Simone's, even with taking rush hour into consideration. Her cottage was only just over an hour's drive away from his flat, after all.

He placed the barely touched beer on the coffee table coaster and checked his watch again whilst he figured out his movements. He could be with her by half past seven, spend all night in her bed and leave at 8:00 a.m. Maybe earlier to miss the bedlam of rush hour traffic, but earlier was OK, too. Now spring had hit, it was glorious to wake up early in the sunlight and have a couple of hours to chill before work.

He thought about burying his face in her dark hair, the sweet smell of her perfume, and running his hand over her soft skin. *Fuck it.* He emptied his beer bottle and stacked it neatly in the recycling bag before rushing back to his car to get to Simone.

Simone

Simone stood frozen in terror, her mouth open. She held her breath and eyed the shadow behind the thick pane of glass in the back door. It didn't move as she stared, wide eyed.

Was it a man's shadow?

Or some sort of tree?

If it were a person, they'd also be able to see her, too. The hairs on the back of her neck raised, and she flicked her arm to the left and snapped off the kitchen light. She counted to ten slowly with her eyes squeezed shut – a technique Theo had taught her in one of their first sessions to manage anxiety alone.

Her ears strained for any noise, but she could only hear the thumping of her own pulse. She pictured Theo sitting in his therapist armchair while she sat on the sofa opposite. She could see the strong curve of his jaw and the worry which lined his forehead sometimes when he studied her. And she could hear his smooth voice telling her it was OK. The Lunar Killer was locked up. He wasn't her attacker, and he was not coming back for her. She opened her eyes and quickly flicked on the kitchen light. The shadow was gone.

She ran to the door and yanked on the handle. It didn't budge.

Phew. Closed, pale-yellow blinds covered the window, and she inserted two fingers between the folds to peer outside to make sure there was no one there.

The garden wasn't as big as she'd originally expected it to be. Country houses always appeared to have large plots of land when you drive by them, but that was not the case with the cottage. This one comprised an old, grey patio made from weathered slabs that no longer sat evenly in the ground. Thin weedlings pushed up from between the cracks. Past the small patio was a square patch of grass about twenty-five feet long that was outlined by trees – all different types and sprouting leaves of different shapes.

Her eyes searched the trees in particular, especially her favourite willow tree slap bang in the middle of the patch of grass. It was stunningly large, and easy to hide behind. But the garden was empty save a small, grey squirrel running up an oak tree. Simone guessed it was an oak tree, at least. Gardening had never been her forte.

She switched her focus to the fence that surrounded the trees and separated it from the adjoining woods. The only access to the garden besides her back door was the four-foot-high fence or the weak gate to the side of the house. Theo said the back garden was private and secure, but really it could have done with a larger fence. Or a sturdier gate, at least.

Still, there was no movement anywhere near the fence. She sighed and turned away, but as she did so another movement caught her eye and her head snapped back. She sucked in a breath as a man appeared from the left-hand side of the garden path, right behind the willow tree. He dressed in a thick winter coat and dark trousers, and faced away from the cottage so his face was hidden. She let go of the blinds and peered through the small slit that was left. An icy fear gripped her heart as he turned around.

He had an axe in his hand.

Simone clamped her hands to her mouth to prevent a scream. He held something huge and brown under his arm. She squinted closer; it looked like logs. He bent down and left the logs in a cubbyhole underneath the barbeque as if he lived in the cottage.

Was this strange man the owner?

Surely he shouldn't be here whilst Theo was renting the place. Anger flooded her at this man ruining her peace, and she opened the window just enough so he could hear her out of it.

"Excuse me, what are you doing here?" She yelled, ready to slam the window shut any second.

The man jumped and turned to search the garden for the mysterious voice. He had a simple, ruddy face and wide eyes. He reminded her of a stereotypical farmer, and was far less threatening from the front. His confused face lit up with a smile once he saw where she was.

"Oh, hi, miss. I'm just filling up the logs for you so you can have a nice fire out 'ere if you wish."

She gave him a piercing look. "Sorry, but who are you exactly?"

"Oh." The man gave a short, jovial chuckle. "I'm sorry, miss. I'm Tom Raddish, the maintenance worker. Or you can call me the skivvy. Either way is fine! If you ever have any issues whilst you're staying 'ere, then Ms Smidtts, the owner, will call me to pop over and 'elp."

"Oh." Simone stared blankly. He seemed nice enough, but he still needed to go away. "I see."

"Is there anything you need before I go, miss?" He didn't seem to take any offence at her bluntness, or even notice she'd been short with him.

"No, thank you," she replied quick as a flash. "Thanks for the logs, though."

"You're welcome, miss. Enjoy your stay. I've got my own key for the side gate." He nodded to her, and she gave a short wave back and closed the window. She watched as he walked over to the left of the garden, where the path led to the only gate, and disappeared.

She could breathe again once he was gone. Her skin tingled all over her body. She shook herself, trying to calm her nerves. But she knew food and wine would settle them better. She made a chicken pot noodle and brought it with her to the living room, curling up on the sofa to eat it whilst watching the TV. Her eyes grew heavy as she watched a murder documentary with a strangely soothing narrator considering the content, and she plonked the remnants of the noodles on the floor and settled onto the sofa. She pulled the soft blanket that sat on the ridge of the sofa over her body and allowed herself to drift off.

She awoke sometime later, rubbing her blurry eyes at the now blank TV. She sat up quickly and looked around. A strange feeling of disorientation overcame her, and not just because she wasn't yet used to the cottage. She hadn't turned the TV off, and yet now it was completely off. Even the standby light was off.

Had she sat on the remote and switched it off?

Even if she had, the standby light would be flashing at her. She sat up and stretched her aching body. She wasn't comfortable enough in the house yet to sleep in the bedroom, but her body was getting sore from multiple nights cramped onto the sofa – comfy as it was. An object on the living room table caught her eye.

And her breath disappeared.

As she'd slept soundly on the sofa, someone had snuck into the cottage and left a gift for her. A small knife with a curved wooden handle and a serrated edge. She jumped up and looked around the room wildly, her stomach in knots. No one was in the living room now.

But someone *was* just outside in the hallway.

Footsteps echoed from the corridor, getting closer to her every second. She couldn't breathe or think straight. She forced herself to breathe in big gulps of air and grabbed the knife, running to the other side of the living room away from the door and away from the intruder. But as the man rounded the living room door, she screamed and fell to the floor.

Theo

Theo pushed open the living room door, excited to see Simone's smiling face at his surprise visit. But her scream almost deafened him. He raced into the living room to see Simone cowering on the floor in the far corner with her eyes shut. She had a knife in her hand and pointed it outwards towards him. His first instinct was to run to her, but shock rooted him in place with his mouth wide open. Simone had never acted like this before. She opened her tear-streaked eyes, which widened once they saw him.

"Theo?" she sobbed.

Her voice shook him into action. "Simone? Hey, hey, hey, it's just me. It's OK."

He crept over to her as he spoke, but she pushed the knife out further in front of her. It shook in her trembling hand. He could overpower her pretty easily, but he took a step back instead.

"Babe, it's me, Theo. You're OK. You're safe. Take a breath. Come on. Count to ten."

Her eyes closed and her breath came in ragged gasps, slowly getting calmer as she counted. Theo carefully wrapped his fingers around hers and pulled the knife away from her with his other hand.

"That's it. Keep going until you get to ten. Count slowly." He watched her face as he put the knife behind him on the coffee table and didn't look away once. After a few seconds, her eyes opened, and she appeared calmer, though her eyes were bloodshot.

"Oh, Theo," she whispered.

"Yes, it's me. I thought I'd surprise you." He smiled at her, hoping she'd be happy he'd turned up. "I'm not sure now if that was a good idea?"

"Oh, thank god." Simone pushed herself forward and fell into his arms. He put one arm around her and stroked her hair with the other. "Someone else has been in here, Theo. I know they have."

"Who's been in here? The owner?" he asked as he kissed the top of her head.

"I don't know, maybe." She took her head off his shoulder and looked up at him. "They left me the knife."

"That knife?" Theo jerked his head in the direction of the coffee table where the knife now lay. Simone followed his look. Her skin was a shade paler than usual, which made her bloodshot eyes look worse. She gulped and nodded as she stared, suddenly transfixed by it. Theo let go of her and pushed himself up off the floor. It was more effort on his knees than he wanted to admit. He stepped over to the table to pick up the knife.

"Put it down," Simone said in a voice that warranted no arguments.

He placed it back down on the coffee table, but continued to examine it. "This was here when we first got here, in the drawer. It's a hunting knife," he said, chewing on the inside of his cheek as he turned to peer at her.

She wrinkled her brow. "It was?"

"Yes, I remember thinking the pattern on the wood was cool." Her face fell and regret hit him. For a therapist, he sure said stupid things sometimes. "Sorry. That was a stupid thing to say when it clearly bothers you."

She shuddered and pushed forward to drag herself up off the floor. "I didn't leave it there." Her face was adamant.

"Is it possible you used it without really looking at it and then noticed it when you woke up? You haven't been sleeping amazingly well for a while now, and that can do all sorts to our brains and thought processes and memories—"

"No. I definitely didn't." Simone cut him off, but she didn't look as sure as she sounded.

"It's possible, though, isn't it?" He tried to get her to see how silly it would be for someone to leave a knife lying around, rather than attacking her with it. Though even he could see that would be a stupid thing to say. Thank god his brain worked sometimes.

"It's also possible that the man I saw in the back garden earlier has been inside," she retorted.

It was Theo's turn to look confused. Nobody else should be anywhere near her. "What? You really saw someone in the back garden? You saw them there tonight?"

Simone's bottom lip trembled, and she bit it hard. Guilt tugged at him, and he sighed. He should have been here for her. It was he who rented it out for her, after all. He walked back over to her, wrapping his arms around her in a way he knew made her feel safe. She sniffed into his shoulder, unable to hold back her tears.

"He said he is the maintenance worker. His name is Tom," she whispered.

He relaxed. "Oh, I see. Well, it's OK. There's no one in here now other than you and me."

"Can we just double-check?" Her muffled voice came through his sleeve.

"Yes, OK. Do you want to wait here?" He let go and looked down at her.

She shook her head vehemently, and Theo led her all over the cottage to check every nook and cranny for any signs of an intruder. No one was hiding anywhere. Nothing was out of place. And he locked all the windows and external doors, and double-checked each one. She even made him check the side gate Tom had left through; it was locked up tight.

There were no more knives lying anywhere. She was safe.

"Do you feel better now?" he asked as they cuddled up on the sofa. He pulled the blanket off the top of the sofa and wrapped her up in it.

"Yes, thanks babe. What would I do without you?"

He ran his finger up and down her arm gently, enjoying the feel of her soft skin.

"Thank you," she mumbled as she fell into another sleep. Theo rested his head on top of hers, holding her tight so she knew she was safe.

Bright light seeped through the curtains at 6:30 a.m. on Friday morning. Theo yawned and stretched out an arm to reach for Simone. But there was a warm, empty space on her side of the bed. He forced one tired eye open, but she wasn't anywhere to be seen.

"Simone?" he croaked, his throat dry. He sat up and took a long gulp of the glass of water from the bedside table to ease his pounding headache. "Simone?"

"Just in the bathroom, babe," Simone called from the en suite. "Be out in a minute."

He stretched again and drank more water to rid his mouth of the unfortunate morning breath that followed drinking too many beers. He smiled as he remembered the previous night. Simone had been more grateful than he could have hoped after they'd moved to the bedroom, and it had certainly been worth the drive.

"Morning." Simone smiled from the en suite doorway with a towel wrapped around her and dark wet hair hanging loose over her breasts.

His eyes widened. "Here, now," he said, pointing to the bed next to him.

She laughed. "Don't be daft, you've got work."

"Damn. What time is it?" he whipped off the covers and grabbed his phone. It was 6:45 a.m., he had fifteen minutes to get showered and leave. "Oh, sorry, babe."

He rushed over to the en suite but couldn't resist grabbing Simone on the way. He wrapped his arms around her and breathed the sweet scent of pink grapefruit. He kissed her neck, and she laughed and pushed him away.

"Get in the shower!" she said as she grinned and walked over to the wardrobe.

By 7:00 a.m. he was back in the bedroom, dressed in a navy suit and white shirt, ready to leave. Simone had only just started to comb her wet hair. God knows what took her so long to dry off. She gave him a strange look, as though she wanted to ask him something but wasn't sure how to say it.

"Yes?" he asked her.

"Can you check the place for me one last time before you leave, please?" she smiled sweetly as she dragged the comb through her wet hair. He walked over and planted a kiss on her soft forehead.

"Of course, I'll be back in a sec."

He strolled around the cottage, starting in the bedrooms and making his way to the living room and kitchen. No one was inside the house, and there were no signs of anything being moved or out of place. He unlocked the back door and took a step outside. The air was fresh, still too early in the year for warm, early mornings, and a breeze carried the musky whiff of earth mixed with sweet spring flowers. Truth be told, he could have sat in the garden at that moment and not moved all day. But he forced himself back inside to say goodbye to Simone, who was still combing her hair in the bedroom.

"It's all clear, nothing suspicious anywhere," he said.

She put down her comb and looked up at him. "Great, thank you. I can rest easy now," she said.

"Come here." Theo walked over and pulled her gently up, wrapping his arms around her and squeezing her tight.

"You're safe and I love you," he whispered.

"I love you, too," she whispered back.

Simone

Simone locked the door behind Theo and stretched. A night in bed made everything so much better. Restless nights on the sofa didn't bode well for anxiety. Thankfully, Theo understood why she acted so insanely paranoid. A smile lined her lips. She'd made the right choice when choosing his office for therapy.

She stood in the corridor, unsure what to do next, with no work to complete. It was strange not working on a story for so long, though nothing truly exciting had happened in Derby since they caught the Lunar Killer. She vaguely remembered he was originally from somewhere in the Peak District, though the murders happened in the city.

There was the odd stabbing, usually thanks to stupid teenagers thinking they were gang members. Or there may be the odd fight in town after too many drinks. All standard city stuff, really. As she looked around the corridor, it was a struggle to remember what she did other than work.

Reading would do. It had been ages since she had the time or inclination to read a good book. She rummaged around in two suitcases before finally finding the book Theo bought for her two weeks prior. It was a sweet romance novel to '*keep her mind off things.*' Not her usual read, but maybe it would be a good idea to stay away from dark thrillers.

She took the book and a strong cup of tea and sat in the back garden on an ancient-looking bench, moving slowly in case it snapped under her weight. Despite looking rotten, it didn't even squeak as it took her weight. She sipped her tea and peered around the garden. It was obvious Tom had mowed the grass recently, but the trees and bushes were untrimmed and gave it more of a natural, wild edge.

A pretty sparrow flew by and landed on the oak tree directly in front of the bench. It sang a high-pitched song, its little white belly moving up and down. A breeze whistled gently through the trees, as if trying to join in with the song. The sparrow appeared oblivious to her sitting so close, and she gazed at the little creature for some time before tearing her eyes away to start the book. As soon as she made a noise, the sparrow flew away, hidden within seconds.

Unexpectedly, the drama of the romance book soon captivated her, and she found herself lost in the main character's poor relationship choices with some questionable women. She almost ignored her phone ringing at lunchtime and pushed it away from her in annoyance, until she realised it was Friday. She threw the book down, cursing herself for forgetting the day, and snatched up her phone.

"Hey, Kerry," Simone answered, thankful she caught it before it went to voicemail. She always welcomed a chat with her best friend, but particularly so this week.

"Hi, baby doll. How are you doing?" Kerry's Essex twang was still strong despite living in Derbyshire since the age of fifteen. She was a runaway, but got herself into university through an access course, and that was where Simone met her for the first time. Fifteen years later, they were closer than ever.

Simone grinned. She'd missed that Essex twang. "I'm doing OK. I'm in the holiday home now. Just for a month until I find a new place."

"Ooh, what's the holiday home like, then? Give me details!"

Simone laughed. Kerry was so dramatic. She gazed over the pretty garden at the stone cottage. "It's beautiful, but it is in the middle of nowhere. Like, it's just me and the birds."

Kerry sighed. Simone could almost see her twirling her hair, as she always did when on the phone. She missed her so much it made her heart ache. "Sounds perfect! Isn't that what you wanted? A place to get away from everyone for a month?"

"Yep. It's exactly what I wanted. I just need to stop my mind wandering sometimes." Simone paused. She'd almost mentioned Tom scaring her but thought better of it. Kerry had enough on her plate learning to cope with schizophrenia. "How are you, anyway?"

"I'm great! I'm going to be out of here within a few months, I reckon."

Simone shot up from the bench. "Really? Like out, out? For good?"

Kerry laughed. "Yes! I think so. I'm really feeling great lately. When I have a bad day, I can recognise it now. I just deal with it rather than spiralling. The doc said it's called insight or something, and if I can tell when I'm having a bad day and deal with it, then I might go home because I can keep safe all by myself."

Simone fist pumped silently and beamed from ear to ear. "Oh, Kerry. I can't tell you how happy that makes me! I'm so proud of you."

"What for? Going bloody bonkers?" Kerry said, laughing again. She was always laughing. It was partly what made her such a great person to be around.

But Simone didn't laugh with her this time. "No! Living with schizophrenia is hard and you're doing amazing. You're gonna do fab when you're out of hospital. You'll see."

"Yeah, well, we'll see. I'm going to ask for leave soon, unaccompanied, so it will just be me out on my own, and once I've proven I can do that, I'll ask to leave. I might ask if I can visit you in the holiday home, if that's OK? They might say no with it being so far away, but I can try."

"Sure, I'll text you the address. I can't wait to see you. Love you."

"Same. Love you, too."

She hung up from Kerry, far too excited to continue with the book. Everything was finally going right. She had an entire month to herself in a fantastic cottage in a beautiful part of the Peak District. Kerry would be home in a few months, and Theo was exactly what she needed. The only twang of anxiety came from not knowing where she was going to live from next month onwards. That really needed sorting.

She put the book back down and grabbed her phone to google a list of available rentals for small properties on the outskirts of Derby. She brought up the list of filters and looked through the options available: garden, parking, bedrooms. Within seconds, she plonked the phone back down again. With no idea what she wanted, other than somewhere safe and not directly in the city, it wouldn't be a simple job. The number of bedrooms didn't matter. It was the security she needed. A built-in security guard would be good.

If only.

She looked to her right, past the garden fence and into the woodland beyond. Maybe a bike ride would be good to clear her head. Then she could focus on finding a new house when she returned. Her bike was in the shed at the front of the cottage, so she went inside to lock up the back door and replace her sandals with a pair of old trainers that were already muddy from previous walks.

She kicked off some larger bits of dry mud by the front door mat before heading to the shed, which stood at the side of the drive. It was a bit of a weird place for a shed, really, but she supposed it didn't matter about people nicking things when they were out in the middle of nowhere. There was no one around to steal anything.

But as she got closer to the shed, her stomach clenched. The padlock on the flimsy door was open, yet she was pretty sure she'd locked it when she'd placed the bike inside. She yanked open the old wooden door and peered in. Everything was still there. The pale-blue mountain bike was right at the front where she left it. Maybe she'd forgotten to lock up.

She grabbed the rubber handle bars and pulled the bike out onto the drive. Now in the Peak District, she had a pang of regret at never having done her driving test. A push bike suffices for living in the city. It saved waiting around for the bus, which was *always* late, and then sitting with a load of strangers.

But she was regretting that choice. The rear tyre of the bike was flat despite changing it recently. How was she going to buy another one now she was stuck in the middle of nowhere?

She turned on the torch of her phone and peered into the shed, searching for something to fix the tyre with. A grin spread across her face as she saw a puncture repair kit hidden under a shelf of junk in the far corner. The owner surely wouldn't notice, and she could replace it before she left, anyway.

She turned the bike around so the wheels faced upwards and leant it against the shed. She inspected the flat tyre. It certainly had zero air in it. She turned the tyre to find the issue, and gasped at what she saw.

There was no puncture in the tyre. Instead, there was a wide rip about five inches long. Something much stronger than running over a nail had clearly torn the jagged edges. Something much more like a hunting knife with serrated edges.

Theo

Theo rubbed his eyes as he pulled into the hardware store car park just off Osmaston Park Road. Early mornings were usually fine for him, but he and Simone hadn't fallen asleep until the early hours and he was feeling the full effects. Thank god his Friday afternoon appointment had been cancelled. Hello, lunchtime finish. Maybe he could see Simone and continue where they left off. He needed a nap first, though.

He struggled to stop yawning as he parked up the Insignia and stretched, slamming the door shut with a bang. The warm summer breeze and dull light of the sunshine against his face helped his sluggishness somewhat. The car park was only half full with it being early afternoon on a Friday, the weekend DIYers wouldn't arrive for a while yet. Thanks to a two-year stint of employment there whilst at university, he could use his insider knowledge to his advantage.

The warm blast of air as he entered the store made him reminiscent of his schooldays. He'd walked through the same doors many times, unsure if he'd ever achieve his goal of becoming a therapist. Not knowing if he'd ever actually feel the joy of quitting and never having to deal with the entitled arsehole customers ever again. But leave he did once he'd independently completed his education. And now he had his very own practice. No thanks to anyone else.

It also meant he knew the layout of the shop extremely well. Most areas stayed the same despite the odd change in stock. So, he walked straight to the rear of the shop to get the rope and wood he needed for a trap for Simone's front door. The fact she trusted him to keep her safe meant a great deal, and he was going to take that responsibility seriously. With no alarm on the rental, he'd make some sort of trap instead that could make a loud noise if anyone opened the front door.

He eyed the different options for rope. It didn't need to be that sturdy. No one was actually after Simone, but she'd feel safer knowing no one could physically get inside without alerting some sort of trap. And ensuring she felt safe after what she endured was his number one priority.

He selected some coarse rope that he knew to be strong and moved to the materials area for wood. Piles of different wood lined the racks, filling his nostrils with its earthy scent. He ran his fingers along the bits of wood on the store shelves, trying to decide which one would be best and would make a good bang against the floor. He selected a thick oak board just as his phone rang out.

He put the board back down and pulled his phone out of his pocket. He grinned when he saw Simone's name flash up, excited to hear her smooth voice and tell her about his plan for the doors.

"Hey, babe," he said, but his grin dropped when he heard her panicked breathing.

"Theo, someone slashed the back tyre on my bike," she said in between gasps. "I told you someone was here last night!"

"Wait, what? How do you know someone slashed it?" asked

Theo, putting down his basket. "Where are you?"

"I'm inside the cottage. There's a full tear in the tyre. It wasn't an accident!" She choked up, holding back tears.

"Hey, listen to me. You need to breathe so we can think this through." He heard her take deep breaths. "If there's a tear in the tyre, any number of things could have happened, right?"

"I thought a nail at first, but it wouldn't make a tear like that," she said in a calmer voice.

"Well, if you caught a nail whilst putting it in the shed and then pushed the bike in, it might rip quite badly," he reasoned.

"Yes, but it's unlikely, isn't it?" she snapped.

"Unlikely things happen, though, babe. What's more likely? That someone who does not know where you are has managed to randomly find you purely to mess with you, or you ripped the tyre on a nail?" Theo noticed a woman giving him a strange look, and stepped over to a quieter corner of the store.

Simone sighed deeply but said nothing.

"Babe? You OK?" he asked.

"Yes. You're right. I don't know why my anxiety is so bad." The sadness in her voice caused an ache in Theo's heart.

"Well, being in the middle of nowhere takes some getting used to if you didn't grow up there."

"What do you mean? You didn't grow up here." she asked in a surprised tone.

Damn. He closed his eyes. She thought he grew up in Derby. Why had he said that?

She didn't sound suspicious. Maybe he'd gotten away with it?

"Oh, you know what I mean. I know how it feels on holidays and stuff." That was partly true, he supposed.

"Come round and tell me all about it?" she said, her voice

back to its sexy smoothness.

"OK. I have no more appointments, but I'm in the hardware store, so I'll pick you up a new tyre and be with you in about two hours? Is that OK? Just stay inside until I get there. You'll be safe."

"Sounds good to me." She sniffed but sounded much calmer. Undeterred by his slip-up, thankfully. He really needed to be more careful and think before he spoke. Even the simplest of lies always had a way of finding their way out. It hadn't mattered when he wasn't close to anyone, but if he was going to stay with Simone, then more of the truth was probably a good idea.

He hung up and walked back over the wood aisle to pick up his abandoned basket. He finished his shopping with the oak beam and new tyre rubber. Determination to make her feel safe took over him. She had no parents, no siblings, and no real friends. He was all she had, and he would not fail her.

Simone

Simone sat on the front steps of the house with her back pushed firmly up against the door. Goosebumps raised on her bare arms thanks to the spring breeze, but she wasn't moving until she could see Theo. The bike lay next to her – the ripped tyre even more obvious now – the sunlight baring down on it.

It took two hours almost to the minute to see Theo's car roll down the driveway. She could see concern etched on his face as the car drew nearer and stopped in front of her. He tried to hide it when he saw her watching him, and turned his frown into a wide smile instead as he jumped out of the car.

"Hi, beautiful," he said, striding towards her. She smiled up at him, and he bent down to kiss the top of her head.

"Thanks for coming over," she replied, pulling herself to her feet with difficulty. Her right thigh had practically seized up. She shook the numbness out of her legs.

"Of course I came over! I always will when you need me. I have a new tyre in the boot for you, too." He nodded his head in the car's direction.

She reached out and stroked his arm. "Thanks, babe. How much do I owe you?"

"It wasn't much. Don't worry about it. Is this the culprit?" He kicked the rear tyre of the bike. Simone nodded. He whistled through his teeth at the tear. "It is pretty big. I bet it was a rat."

"A rat?" Simone grimaced. "You really think so?"

"Yeah, they have massive, sharp teeth, you know. They do all kinds of damage. And sheds are the perfect place for a rat to hide. Don't look so disgusted! You're always going to get rats in the countryside."

"How do you know so much about everything?" Simone asked. "You always seem to have the answer."

He laughed. "There're loads of things I know nothing about! I just know about manly things and useless facts, mainly," he said with a wink.

He popped the bike upside down and set to work on replacing the tyre whilst Simone stood awkwardly next to him, unsure how to help. Her dad hadn't lived long enough to show her how to do such things. She longed for him to be here now.

"I'll make us some lunch," she said to Theo, and disappeared into the house.

She headed down the corridor to the kitchen and opened the fridge door, mulling over the contents. Eventually, she grabbed a box of eggs, cheese, milk, and butter and made two large omelettes. Just as she was serving them up, the front door closed and Theo reappeared in the corridor.

"All fixed," he said. "Smells good in here!"

Simone laughed. "No one thinks eggs smell good! It will taste good, though. I promise. Here." She handed him a large blue plate with the folded omelette.

"Thank you. Have I told you how much I love you today?" He put the plate down and pulled her close, kissing her cheek.

She leant into him, enjoying the tickle of his soft stubble

against her cheek. It had grown just long enough not to irritate her skin. "I love you, too. Now, eat your lunch before it goes cold."

"Oh, I quite like it when you tell me off." He grinned.

She swatted him away playfully, dragged a chair noisily across the wooden floor and pointed at it. He plonked the omelette down and sat, motioning for her to sit next to him as he took his first bite.

"Do you feel better now?" he asked.

"Yes. I guess I'm just adding things up wrong because of nerves," she answered.

"Exactly. Just because it looked like it was the same knife used on you doesn't mean it was."

Simone stopped chewing and stared at him, her eyes wide. "What did you say?"

"The knife from last night. With it looking like the same one that—" He stopped talking mid-sentence, and his fork clattered to his plate. His mouth still open, he reached out to hold her hand. "I'm so sorry, babe. I shouldn't have brought it up. Are you OK?"

Simone's stomach turned, but she forced herself to swallow the food in her mouth. It stuck in her dry throat, and she got up to pour a glass of water.

"Simone? Are you OK?"

"I was until you mentioned the knife."

"I'm so sorry honestly I didn't mean—"

"It's not that you mentioned it," her voice wobbled. She cleared her throat. "But how do you know it was the same knife used in the attack? Because I've never told you that."

Theo

Theo put a hand to his stomach as if Simone had punched him hard in the gut with a heavy frying pan. He didn't respond straight away but peered at her, trying to figure out what to say and how to feel. He wanted to reach past his hurt and be understanding, like he would be in a therapy session with a client. But Simone was no longer a client. She was his entire world. And he struggled to grasp his anger. He gripped his knife and fork.

"Jesus, Simone. Do you really still not trust me after all this time? What about the months of therapy sessions? Or the late-night phone calls I always answer? I run straight to you whenever you have a problem. I don't know what else I can do to win your trust?"

She didn't answer. But her bottom lip wobbled, and she bit it tightly. She rarely cried in front of him. He placed his cutlery back on the plate and fiddled with his ring. His anger ebbed away.

"You told me in a therapy session," he said, his voice still cooler than usual. He didn't want to fall out with her, but the disappointment seeped into his voice involuntarily.

She swallowed. "When? Which therapy session was it?"

He resisted the urge to reach a hand out to comfort her,

knowing she would push him away in that moment. He thought about their many conversations, and one night in particular where she had laid her heart bare.

"After you told me about the death of your parents," he told her.

She sucked in a breath and looked away. He knew the murder of her father was even more of a sore subject than last year's attack, and he would never usually bring it up unless she mentioned it first. She'd probably have turned to him if he were still alive and have no need for Theo. He would bring back her dad for her in a heartbeat if he could, but he couldn't deny a tiny part of him was glad she turned to him and him alone. He was all she had, and he would have done anything to make her feel better. Even if she had hurt him through silent accusations.

She turned back to face him, her eyes now clear of tears. "I don't remember telling you about the knife," she said.

"There's no other way I would know. Do you want me to get my notes? Would that make you feel more comfortable?" He hoped he didn't sound sarcastic. If that was what it took to prove himself to her, then that was fine by him.

She stared at him for a moment with a strange look in her eyes and then shook her head. "No, I believe you. I just get confused sometimes." She reached out a hand to him and he gripped it. "I'm sorry."

"Don't worry. No need to ever say sorry for getting confused. Are you sure you don't want my notes? I just want you to know you can trust me. I want you to feel safe around me," he urged.

"I do feel safe around you," she answered without hesitation.

"Good." He pulled her forward into a bear hug and kissed the top of her soft hair. She leaned into him and wrapped her arms around his middle. He breathed in her sweet scent and then pulled her head up towards him, kissing her softly on the lips.

Their eyes locked, and he kissed her deeper. Desperate to make his love for her known. But she pulled away and took a step back. He looked up, wondering what he'd done wrong. But she was smiling at him whilst lifting her top up inch by inch. He grinned back, but was in no mood to wait. He grabbed her hand and led her inside to the bedroom where they stayed for the rest of the day, and finally, she let him be in control for once.

Simone

The sparrow awoke Simone the next morning. She opened her eyes to him perching right outside the bedroom window. He peered in through the gap in the curtain as if he wanted to watch over her. He sang his spring melody once more, and it travelled through the open window.

Simone sat up in bed. She never opened the window at night. Theo's quiet snores stopped, and she turned to look at him. He opened one eye and squinted at the window.

"Close the window, babe. Damn birds," he moaned.

"I didn't open it last night, did you?" she asked.

"No idea. Come give me a cuddle." He reached an arm out to drag her back to him. She lay down, still staring at the sparrow who continued to sing.

"Oh god, he's so noisy," Theo moaned again.

Simone pushed Theo's arm away and ripped off the cover. She snuck over to the window and peered at the bird for a moment. He tilted his head and stared right at her. She shivered. It looked like the same sparrow from the garden, but they all looked the same really with their little brown heads, beady dark eyes and white bellies. She reached a hand up to close the window, and in a flash, he flew away. The bedroom faced the back of the house and she examined the rest of the garden. There was nobody there. It must have been Theo who opened the window at some point. They had gotten pretty hot and sweaty last night. She could feel the bruises on her legs without even checking them. She shivered again at the thought of anyone else sneaking into the bedroom and opening the window while they slept.

Nope. It was definitely Theo.

"Come back," Theo groaned. He reached out a hand towards her.

"I'm coming," she replied, walking back to him. "It must have been you with the window."

"Yes, it must have been me." He pulled her towards his chest and wrapped his arms around her. "In fact, I know it was me. I was awake for a while last night after you fell asleep. There's something I have to tell you."

Simone looked up at him, immediately wary of his tone. He kissed her on the top of her head.

"Go on…" She tried to ignore the fear brewing inside her stomach.

"I was awake for a while because I had to take a call not long after you fell asleep. To cut a long story short, I need to go to Ireland to see my folks."

"Oh, I never knew they lived in Ireland." Simone looked away so he couldn't see the disappointment on her face. "When are you going?"

He cleared his throat. "Yeah, they moved there a couple of years ago. My stepdad is from there originally. I need to go today. I booked a flight last night while you were sleeping."

"Today?" Simone shot up, panicked at the thought of being in the house alone with no one nearby to call. She knew she was safe when Theo was with her. If he wasn't there, then the anxiety would come flooding back.

"Yes, but only for a couple of days." He sat up too, looking at her with concern. "It's just because my mum hasn't been well with her anxiety. My stepdad wants me to have a chat with her to calm her down. He said she needs me."

Simone said nothing until she was sure the lump in her throat had disappeared. "Your mum has anxiety?"

Theo nodded. "She's always suffered in bouts. It rises in intensity when she's worried about something. That's why I started studying counselling. She sort of inspired me to help people, and I wanted to help her, too."

"I'm sorry she's not feeling well. So, is she worried about something now? Is there anything I can do to help?"

"Well, nobody knows what it is she's worried about, but she seems to be focused on something, yes. She isn't sleeping or eating properly, and she's losing her temper over nothing. So, until we know what it is, if there even is anything specific, it's hard to know who can help."

A need to beg him not to go grabbed her, but she pushed it away. If he said his mum needed him, then that was that.

"OK, I'll miss you," she replied, and climbed out of bed. She headed over to the en suite to jump in the shower. She could think in there ... and cry.

"Are you sure you're going to be OK?" he called from the bed.

She smiled softly. "I was fine before you came into my life, Mr Therapist, and I'll be fine for a couple of days on my own. Don't you worry about me."

She heard him laugh. "Of course, you will be. You don't need me at all."

By lunchtime, Theo had left, along with the sandwiches she packed up for him. And Simone was all alone once again. She sat in the garden on the old picnic table with her laptop sitting precariously on top. The only noise was from the sparrows fluttering from tree top to tree top, singing to protect their territory or attract a mate. Though a similar-looking dunnock hopped around on the ground near the bench, searching for prey.

The day was unusually sultry for spring, with the sun being much stronger than it had been all week. She held out her bare arms and let the rays warm her pale skin. A tan always made things better. Or it would at least improve her look if nothing else.

After a few minutes of soaking up the sun, she lowered her arms and forced herself to concentrate despite the glorious weather. She had a house to find. Maybe even a forever home. She smiled at the thought. A home surely wasn't too much to ask for. There must be a perfect, affordable home nestled somewhere within the long lists of snapshots.

She scrolled through one such list on the most well-known estate agency website. She checked the essentials of each listing before bothering to look at the pictures, after an early mistake of falling in love with the images of a beautiful two-bedroomed house which was way too far from the office.

Two bedrooms would be enough, but it needed to be far enough from the city that she felt safe at night, and it needed to be close enough to the city that work was easy to get to. Kerry would be in the city when she left the hospital, and she would need Simone to help her get settled. So, it had to be close to Kerry as well.

A modern apartment caught her eye, and she scanned the

details under the heading. It had two bedrooms and gated entry, and a maintained rear garden for tenants to share. It looked so perfect she barely heard the twig snap. It took a few seconds to register what the noise was, but once it did, her head shot up. And she stared right into the eyes of the sparrow.

The little bird cocked his head to one side, and for once he wasn't singing. He stared straight at her as if he wanted to say something. Simone shivered. And as she opened her mouth to tell it to go away, it suddenly flew up and hovered in front of her face. It flew straight over the oak tree and into the woodland.

Simone stared after the bird, and just underneath where it disappeared, she saw it.

A crouched shadow moved from one tree to the next.

She stood, every hair on her body raised despite the warmth of the sun. Was it an animal?

Or a man cowering down to hide as he watched her?

Backing away from the bench, she didn't take her eyes off the tree where the shadow disappeared. She didn't look away until the handle of the back door dug into the small of her back, when she turned and fled into the house. She slammed the door behind her and fumbled with the key. Her hands shook so much it was hard to turn the key, but she forced them to work eventually and locked it up tight. She leant against the door, sucking in air, and closed her eyes.

Count to ten. It was nothing. It was an animal. He isn't here.

She grabbed her phone to call Theo, before remembering he'd be on a flight on his way to Ireland. It wasn't a long flight, but there was no way he'd be off the plane that quickly. She typed in the hospital's number instead and was thankful that a receptionist answered within three rings. She asked to speak to

Kerry. Just hearing her friendly voice and Essex twang would help.

"I can't put you through to her directly, but I'll ask her to call you back as soon as she can," the receptionist said in a short tone. She was efficient, but far from friendly.

Simone hung up but held the phone tight to ensure she didn't miss Kerry returning her call. She stepped over to look out of the blinds of the kitchen window. She could just about see the spot where the shadow had moved. But nothing was there now. She stayed rooted to the spot. If she watched long enough, he'd have to come out. She stared at the spot for a full two minutes, right until her phone vibrated and made her jump.

"Hello, Kerry?"

"Hi, doll. Are you OK?" Kerry rushed the words out, as she always did when concerned about something.

"Yes, fine! I wondered if I could ask you something about another friend of mine," Simone replied as calmly as she could, still fixated on the spot where the shadow had been.

"Another friend? Are you cheating on me?" Kerry laughed.

"Never!" Simone forced a laugh, too. "It's just someone from work. She's been acting strange lately. I'm worried about her. I wanted some advice."

"Oh, why are you worried about her?"

Simone faltered. "I don't really know how to explain it. She thinks she's seeing a man in her house, but whenever someone checks, there's no one there."

"Oh, god. OK. How many times and what dates? What happened recently to make her feel like that? Has she seen a doctor?" Kerry was instantly in journalist mode with her questioning. Simone wondered if she was taking notes. She probably was if the hospital allowed her to have a pen. They hadn't allowed Simone to bring a pen into the session when she'd visited last year. Kerry only allowed that one visit, too independent to accept any further help.

"Kind of. She's spoken to a therapist. She speaks to him about anxiety. No one has mentioned hallucinations yet... But I'm worried that's what it might be."

"Well, it could be. Does she ever hear things?"

"No. I mean, I don't think so," Simone added quickly.

"Well, I know from experience, traumatic experiences can cause hallucinations. So, if there's really no one there, then I would suggest she speak to her therapist about hallucinations. They can be completely real to the person seeing them. I still don't trust my own eyes sometimes."

Simone finally pulled her gaze away from the empty woodland spot. God, she was selfish sometimes. Kerry had been through enough.

"You're doing so well, though, Kerry. I can't wait to see you in the flesh outside the hospital!"

"Me neither! I'm gonna squeeze you to death. You know that, right?"

Simone laughed. "Not if I get you first. Have you got a date yet for your leave?"

"No, but I will have it soon. It's nerve wracking, really. I'll have to look after myself again!"

"We can look after each other, don't worry. Love you."

Simone hung up from Kerry, overwhelmed with excitement. She would be out of that damn hospital soon. Suddenly, being scared over a shadow seemed completely ridiculous. Maybe being out in the countryside didn't suit her, after all. Maybe she needed a tad more noise. And less bloody sparrows.

No more shadows appeared as the hours passed and the sky

turned to dusk. The earlier shadow in the trees must have been nothing more than imagination, or that damn bird creeping her out with its beady, black eyes. She returned to the living room and pushed most of the deer-emblazoned cushions on the floor so she could stretch out properly on the sofa. She switched the TV to the same serial killer documentary she'd fallen asleep to the night before with the relaxing narrator and pulled down a grey fleece blanket from the top of the sofa to tug over her body.

The living room was cool, and despite the soft blanket, she considered moving to turn the heating on, but Theo had put it on a schedule, so she woke up toasty and she didn't want to mess that up. Another thing her dad would have shown her how to do. Despite the subject of the documentary, she closed her eyes and felt quite relaxed. The narrator's voice continued in the background.

'Walter Smidtts killed three women before the police found him. They linked the bank card found near the third victim to an address in the quiet Derbyshire Peak District.'

Simone's eyes flew open. She knew that name. Walter Smidtts, aka the Lunar Killer. The camera panned to a familiar-looking village. She racked her brain. Walter Smidtts lived near Derby, but where? She squinted at the TV, trying to see which village it was, praying it wasn't Edale.

'Past the town of Edale lies a remote cottage.'

She shot up as the screen changed and showed an image of a pretty stone cottage surrounded by woodland. It had a small driveway with a rickety shed out front, and a back garden covered in trees.

The very cottage she was sitting in.

Simone flew off the couch, one hand gripping her stomach

to keep the nausea at bay. She paced the floor. A serial killer's home. *She was in a serial killer's home,* alone, and with night time fast approaching.

The narrator's voice was no longer as soothing, and she grabbed the remote to turn the documentary off. She picked up her laptop from the floor. It vaguely crossed her mind that maybe reading about him wasn't the best idea, but she had to *do* something. She clutched her stomach tighter with one hand as she scrolled through an article with the other.

She knew all about Walter Smidtts's crimes. The entire country did. It was the biggest news story in the UK at the time, and it had fascinated everyone in the office. It wasn't her story to write about for the rag, but she'd read loads of other articles. Jenny had joked that Simone was obsessed with him. And now it was all coming back to her.

She'd completely forgotten where he was from; his crimes and ultimately his trial consumed the articles rather than where he lived. She remembered something about the Peak District, but it covered almost three hundred miles of land. Not for one second had it occurred to her that he might have originated from Edale.

She continued to read through the article to remind herself of the gory details. He'd beat young women in their late teens or early twenties. The women always had medium to long dark hair. Initially, he would grab them from the street and attack them, but let them go. He didn't even rob them. But he watched them. He followed them. He saw them attempt to get their lives back together. And four weeks later, he kidnapped, tortured and murdered them. The twenty-eight-day cycle is where his name came from, the Lunar Killer. He was a sick individual. But they'd caught him, and she knew he was locked away. There's no way he'd have been let out.

She looked around the living room. Is this what it looked like when he lived here? Had he sat on this sofa? Did he choose the cushions? A chill ran through her, and she picked up the blanket to wrap it around her shoulders.

A mugshot of Smidtts stared out from the laptop. She remembered it being all over the news. You could barely look anywhere without seeing his face. He was bald with a large nose and gaunt cheeks, not handsome but not particularly ugly either. He was just an average-looking bloke. How many 'normal' looking people had she passed on the street who actually hid such dark thoughts? How many killers had she walked by in her life without knowing it?

She jumped as her phone vibrated from the coffee table. Theo's name flashed up, but she didn't move. He could wait. She needed to read. She went back to flicking through the many tabs she now had open about Smidtts.

Police arrested Smidtts two years ago, and he was now a resident of Adrenna Psychiatric hospital according to the article. It also stated that he lived with his mum in the Peak District. It was her house, not his. They found no bodies in the house or on the grounds. Simone shivered again and looked around as if his mum was still there. She must have been so sickened by him she couldn't stay in the cottage, and instead rented it out as a holiday home. She could've stated on the advert it was a bloody serial killer's lair.

Slamming the laptop closed, she rushed to the kitchen to grab the bottle of wine. Drinking was the last thing she should do, but she filled a glass to the top regardless and gulped it down. This whole cottage thing was a stupid idea. She could stay somewhere else. Maybe get a hotel room for a few nights at least. But she only had enough money for a couple of nights at the most, and she'd never get a deposit together for a new place if she spent her money on a hotel. She grabbed her phone from the coffee table. She needed to know what Theo would do.

Theo

T heo sunk into the doughy, black sofa in his mother's living room. It surprised him she could get back up off it with the arthritis in her knees and her ever-increasing weight. She stared down at the floor and refused to look at him. But even in the dull light, the pale skin and sweaty sheen of her face made it obvious she wasn't well. Quite pathetic, really.

"I've got nothing to tell you." She shrugged. "You can't fix everyone, son. Just leave me alone."

Theo covered his face with both hands and took a deep breath before looking back at her. Her stubbornness was unmatched, and he'd never had as much patience with family as he did with clients. His useless mother didn't deserve his help. Truth be told, he was more bothered about why Simone hadn't called him back.

What if something had happened to her, and she was in that cottage all alone?

It would be all his fault, too. Seeing as it was his idea to go to the Peak District in the first place. And then he rented it out for her and left her all alone. A sinking feeling hit the bottom of his stomach. He had to make sure she was OK.

"I'm going to make a call and give you some time to think it over," he said as calmly as he could manage. "When I get back, we'll talk about it some more."

He stood, looking at her for a response. She didn't even blink. He shook his head and marched into the kitchen. Its garish yellow-and-pink decor gave him an instant headache.

"I'll make us tea," he yelled back through to her and flicked on the bright-pink kettle so she couldn't hear him talking to Simone. He didn't need questions about who she was. There was no way he'd be bringing her anywhere near his family. Not now and not in a million years. She'd run a mile. Hell, he would run away from them if he could. Maybe he would one day.

He pulled out his phone to call her again, but Simone's name flashed up before he could bring up her number. The butterflies in his stomach fluttered as they always did when he spoke to her. Even now they'd been dating for a while. Well, three months, but it felt more like three years. He cleared his throat and hit the answer button.

"Hi, babe, are you OK?" he asked.

"No, not really." Simone sniffed as though she were crying.

Theo leant against the kitchen counter with one hand on his forehead. He steeled himself for bad news. "What's wrong? I tried to call... I was worried about you."

She sniffed again. "I was watching some stupid documentary on TV and it was talking about a serial killer, and next thing there was a picture of this house on the TV! Do you remember Walter Smidtts from a couple of years ago? It was *his* house, Theo. Still is his house! Or his mum's, I'm not sure. He's in some mental hospital for serious psychopaths."

Theo couldn't say anything. It was as if his brain had stopped working, and he could no longer think or move.

"Theo? Did you hear me?" Simone's voice brought him back to reality.

"A serial killer?" he whispered, struggling to form the words. He swallowed. "Are you sure? Maybe the cottage just looked similar? They do all look the same to me. Little stone things surrounded by trees."

Simone hesitated. He could just about hear her swallow and another sniff.

"Babe, are you sure?" he asked again.

She took a deep breath. "Yes, I'm sure. I googled it after and saw the image. It was definitely this house."

"Maybe googling it wasn't such a good idea. No good ever comes from that. You can't believe half the stuff you see online."

"I don't like it, Theo. I know he's locked away, but he beat them in the street and then let them think they were safe" – she sniffed again – "and *murdered* them a month later. Who the hell does that? What if that happens to me?"

Theo flushed red with rage at the thought of someone hurting her. "Your attack was seven months ago, Simone. He isn't coming for you. Look, I'm coming home," he said in a voice that warranted no arguments. "No one is going to hurt you. Do you hear me?"

"What about your mum? She needs you right now," she tried to argue. It was just like Simone, always thinking of others before herself. That's why she needed someone to take care of her, someone to put her first. She needed him more than his weak excuse for a mother.

"She'll be fine. She *is* fine. Trust me. I'll look at flights and get back to you soon, babe. Just stop freaking yourself out, OK? Even if it was his house, they arrested him years ago. He isn't hanging around. Stop googling."

Simone sighed. "OK," she said in a much calmer voice.

The line disconnected, and Theo pulled up a new tab on his phone to check the next available flight time. Maybe there'd be extra flights with it being Saturday. He tried to swallow the panic threatening to take over every inch of his body. He'd known the cottage was a bad idea deep down, but it was the only affordable option. Now he needed to get to her as soon as possible. Before she started digging too deep.

Simone

Despite a small voice insisting alcohol wasn't a good idea, Simone rummaged around in the cupboards for a larger wine glass, though she happily could have drunk it out of the bottle. The powerful smell of wood clung to her nostrils and made her nauseous stomach turn. She held her breath and opened the final cupboard. Pint glasses teetered on the edge of the top shelf. One of those would have to do. Not exactly classy, but no one was around to judge.

Kerry would have laughed and grabbed a pint glass with her if she were here.

She filled the glass halfway and took a large swig. It was hard to swallow at first and made her tongue spasm, but the second swig went down easier. She took another deep breath. Theo would be on his way soon. She had to keep it together. She had to breathe and control the anxiety like he taught her.

She looked down at the pint glass, and couldn't help but smile. It brought memories of student life flooding back, drinking from any kind of glass that was around. She felt the same sad fondness she always felt when reminiscing about student life – her enjoying life with Kerry and not giving two cares about the world around them. They were young and invincible. Their current issues were not even a consideration. Life was so much harder without her laughter, but it wouldn't be long until she was back. Maybe they could party with pint's of wine together.

She took her wine pint, and the dregs left in the bottle, and went back to the living room, switching on a chick flick this time. Simone was no longer intrigued by relaxing serial killer documentary narrators. As she watched the daft woman and her clumsy suitor fall in love, her thoughts turned to Theo. He was always so calm and collected. A regular modern-day saviour.

The film became nothing but background noise as her mind wandered and the wine took hold. Quicker than usual, probably thanks to the glass. She'd never been in love before. Not unless you counted Micky Sarve when she was sixteen. A popular boy in school with a nose piercing and a rich daddy. But that didn't last long. He was so nice for weeks on end after her father died, trying to get her to kiss him in the park after school on their 'dates.' He begged her for a naughty picture, and after about two months, she'd fallen for him hook, line and sinker. She texted him a picture of her breasts. He showed it to everyone in school. Her face wasn't even in it, but that didn't matter. Everyone knew it was her. That had been the end of her and Micky, and he'd died in a car crash six months later. He'd probably have grown to be an abusive dickhead, anyway.

Trusting men after that had always been hard, but it was different with Theo. She *knew* Theo. The real Theo. Not some face he showed to others. Her phone vibrated, and she turned to pick it up. The text was blurry thanks to the lack of glasses and too much wine, but with a squint she could see it was a message from Theo.

'Don't worry, I had an idea. We'll contact the landlord in the

morning and get your money back. Then you can go somewhere else. I'll help you pack. Don't panic. It will be OK. Love you.'

Simone smiled and continued to sip her wine. It wasn't long before her bleary eyes closed and she slipped into a deep sleep on the sofa. She went back to the past in her dreams, mainly about Dad. Not of his untimely death in front of her own young eyes, but of their cuddles on the sofa, and him tickling her whenever he came home from the pub and making her laugh like crazy. He was so protective, keeping her safe from everything. He'd always seemed so invincible, yet a single stab wound was all it took to end his life and change hers forever.

Theo

Theo shivered and pulled his coat around him tighter. Cold weather rarely bothered him. But the empty children's park in front of him was in the middle of a wide, grassy verge surrounded by tall houses, and the wind whipped around inside the grounds as if in a mini vortex. A bit like his own feelings.

Mum wasn't any better. But he couldn't leave Simone to suffer. And if his mother didn't want him there anyway, what was the point of sticking around?

He pulled out his phone and checked the time: 10:00 a.m. already. The day was flying by. He was going to ask face to face if he could get the money back for the holiday home, but lost his nerve at the last minute. Hence why he was now at the park with his phone to his ear.

His knee bounced up and down as he waited for them to answer. His gut had churned all night at not being able to hold Simone when she was scared and all alone. The next flight wasn't until 2:00 p.m. the next day, so he would have to wait. Visiting Mum was a mistake. There was clearly no genuine risk from a killer who was locked away, but there was no surprise Simone was scared by the whole thing.

All he could do was attempt to get her away from the cottage.

And preferably, away from the internet before she went too far. There were things she didn't need to know. Well, one day he might tell her. Maybe. But definitely not yet. She wasn't ready.

The phone continued to ring out, and he considered hanging up. But speaking to the owner was his only option to get Simone into a different place. He couldn't afford to send her anywhere otherwise. The month in the cottage had swallowed up his meagre savings.

Just as he lowered the phone to end the call, a gruff voice answered, which made the churning in his gut increase tenfold. It was the voice of a woman who'd smoked forty cigarettes a day for decades.

"Yes, hi, it's me," he replied in a dejected voice. He already knew what the answer would be. This was pointless.

"What do you want now?" came the annoyed reply. "I thought I'd gotten rid of you."

Theo took a deep breath and shut his eyes tight. He had to try for Simone's sake.

"I need a refund for the cottage. The woman who I rented it out to has found out it belonged to Walter."

"And?" the woman replied. "People normally like that. It gives them a thrill."

"*And* she doesn't want to stay there anymore." Theo's voice was rising already. He clenched his jaw.

"Well, it's not exactly a secret, is it? Everyone local knows what happened, and you said she's from Derby. People come all over to stay in a serial killer's house. It's well advertised."

"Yes, well. She wasn't aware. Derby isn't that local. Half of them never even visit the Peak District."

"You knew, though. Why did you not tell her before she

moved in?"

"She's been through a lot and was desperate for some peace. There was nowhere else available for a full month. Not in that area, anyway. So, I didn't want to mention it to her. I didn't know he'd be on some stupid documentary she was watching."

The woman snorted. "The way I see it, that's your problem, not hers. That mess is all your fault. She's free to leave and I'll place it back as available online, but you won't be getting your money back."

"Where's your empathy? It's no wonder Walter turned out like he did with a mother like you!" he spat and hung up the phone before she could reply, launching his phone across the field.

He sat back down on the bench with a thud and put his head in his hands, trying to think where he could get some money from for Simone. Being a private therapist wasn't as lucrative as one might think, being hard to advertise and keep clients. He barely had enough money to cover his own extortionate bills, never mind renting another place out for Simone. Giving her most of his savings as a one-off was fine – he would do anything to help her no matter the cost. But if his money was gone, what else could he do? She was stuck there for now. He just hoped she stopped digging. For her own safety and his.

Simone

Simone awoke with a start on the sofa. It was Sunday morning and harsh daylight seeped into the room through the crack where the curtains didn't quite meet each other. She put her hand up to shield her tired eyes from the light. But as usual her sweet dreams had turned into dark nightmares, and the vision of her father's death still danced on her eyelids. The pain etched on his face as the knife slid into him would forever scar her memories, but it didn't fade with age like real scars.

If only the murder was just a nightmare and Dad was still alive. Life would have turned out so differently. Dad would be around to protect her. She put a hand to her chest to squash the ache in her heart and sat up properly, rubbing her stinging eyes hard to get rid of the lasting visions. Then she remembered about Smidtts and opened her eyes wide.

The serial killer's lair.

The cottage felt different now. The warmth had disappeared, replaced with a feeling of being somewhere *wrong*. As if she was somewhere no one should ever be. Did the evil Smidtts sleep on this very sofa? She almost fell in her rush to stand and get away from it. She stared at the sofa from the other side of the living room as if it might come alive. Her phone was on the floor next to it. *Damn* it.

Creeping back over to the sofa, she grabbed her phone from the floor before fleeing to the other side of the room. She shook her head and laughed at her nerves. This is not how she'd imagined behaving at thirty-three years old. She walked into the kitchen. Everything smelled new and fresh in there, so he'd probably never sat at the table. She leaned against the counter and checked her phone for messages from Theo about the landlord. There was nothing, which was strange. She opened her messages to double-check she hadn't accidentally clicked on a new message and made it disappear from her notifications, but there was nothing sitting in there either. Not even his daily good morning text. She checked the time. It was 10:30 a.m., so he should be well awake by now. Unlike her – and most normal people – Theo hated sleeping in late, even on weekends. He was so et in his little ways. God help anyone who placed a cup down without using a coaster in front of him. She called his number and walked over to the kettle, filling it with water as his phone rang out.

But there was no answer. She plonked the kettle on its base and flicked on the switch. Theo always answered his phone. Maybe he was on a flight already? But surely it wouldn't ring out if he was.

Wow, her nerves were on fire. He was probably just busy. She needed to relax. Her muscles were all so tight. She yawned and stretched out her aching limbs until the pain in her right leg died down. It always ached the most in the morning when her body was still stiff. She lifted the loose edge of her pale, silk pyjama shorts and traced her fingers along the angry red scar at the top of her thigh. She'd been lucky to survive the hunting knife going into her thigh. Thank god it had missed her major artery, or she would have bled too quickly to be saved.

Her lips stuck together, too dry from being greedy with the wine the night before, so she made do with a glass of water whilst she waited for the kettle to boil. As she reached the sink, a flash of something out of place caught her eye, and she stared down the corridor toward the front door. There was something on the floor in front of the door. Something white. She put down her glass and stepped into the hall, not daring to go too far or to move too quickly. On the floor lay a white piece of paper. An icy fear grabbed her heart.

Yet again someone was sneaking around as she slept.

She strained her ears but heard only silence. Maybe she was overreacting, and the paper had fallen down from the side table or something. She walked over to the note. Each step down the hallway felt twice as long as usual thanks to the pain in her head from too much wine. She reached for the paper and bent down to pick it up. The first side was blank, but the icy fear gripped harder when she turned it over and saw the four words written in thick black letters.

'I know you lied.'

Theo

Theo greeted the familiar winding road to the cottage by almost crashing into a tractor as he flew around the corner. He slammed on his breaks and swerved past as the driver, who threw him an angry look. And probably a few curse words. Theo muttered a few choice words to himself and carried on.

He certainly hadn't missed that part of country life since moving to the city. There were some small things he missed from his childhood. He enjoyed his hazy memories of summer days and mossy trees and made-up games. But that was before Dad died and Mum turned into a sour bitch.

It was a fantastic place for a little one to grow up in. Adventure lay around every corner. The gigantic tractors were amazing to look up at as a little boy. Along with his brother, he would point and shout in excitement whenever they saw one. He climbed on top of one as a teenager after a few too many stolen beers, and broke his collarbone when he swiftly fell back off it. But like most things in life, the fun wore off as an adult and they were nothing but an inconvenience these days.

He pulled back to the left side of the road and straightened up. He didn't get back up to speed, choosing instead to stick to forty mph. And even less through the bends. He was lost in his own thoughts as the hills whizzed by. Thankfully, the roads were quiet and other than the odd annoying cyclist, he saw nobody else. He could probably move back to the Peak District for Simone. Especially when she wanted children, which he knew she did one day. She said she wanted three, all boys. He hadn't told her he'd grown up around here as one of two boys. At first, she was nothing but a client anyway, and he always lied to clients about his own life. The last thing he needed was an obsessive client to be digging deeper into his life.

But now she was so much more than a client, and she deserved the truth. The full truth. Just as soon as she recovered, and was strong enough to handle it. That way, it wouldn't matter if she dumped him. If she was strong enough, she'd be OK without him, anyway. He wouldn't have to worry. Though he felt a harsh twang in his chest at the thought of her no longer needing him.

He pulled off before the traffic lights which led to the nearby campsite and onto Pickford Lane, a straight stretch of road. Well, it wasn't much of a road. It was barely more than a trail, and was just big enough to fit one vehicle. The cottage came into view at the top of the lane, and he picked up speed despite the precarious size of the trail. All he could think about was finally seeing Simone.

He pulled into the drive and sat in the car for a moment, ignoring his desperate desire to see her. He picked up his phone and pressed the 'on' button repeatedly. But no luck; it was completely dead. He hadn't texted her before he left, and the last thing he wanted was to scare her again. She couldn't be afraid of him.

He threw his phone onto the passenger seat in frustration.

Everyone was so reliant on technology these days, and when it didn't work, it was as if the world couldn't function. Maybe he needed to go without for a week. Maybe he and Simone could both go without for a week. They could stay in the tranquil cottage together, the two of them alone with no phones, no TV and no internet. Bliss. But he was pretty sure she would never go for that.

He wondered what it would take to convince her to give up her phone and laptop as he exited the Insignia and strolled over to the front door. The birds were so noisy in spring, but he was glad for their songs as it broke the otherwise eerie silence. It didn't surprise him to find the door locked. He gently knocked on it and stood back. He watched the tiny birds fly around and call to each other. Or were they warning each other? He never cared much for birds. Christ, they were annoying. He'd never noticed how loud they were as a kid.

He stepped forward and knocked again. *Where the hell is she?* It wasn't like there were many places she could just pop out to with no bike or car. He sighed and shoved a hand in his jeans pocket, leaving his forefinger poking out to tap it against the pocket of the denim. But there was no answer from Simone. The only noise was still those damn birds.

He pulled his hand out of his pocket and stepped over to the living room window. The curtains were closed, but they were too small for the large window, and there was a small gap where they met. He shielded his eyes from the sunlight to peer inside through the crack. A grey blanket lay strewn on the floor next to the sofa alongside some cushions. Simone's laptop was open on the coffee table. He couldn't see her phone or shoes. Maybe she'd gone for a walk. There wasn't much else she could be doing.

He swallowed his annoyance and walked back to the car. Theo sat in silence for a moment as he watched the cottage. Nothing happened. Simone didn't suddenly appear from any of the windows or at the front door. But as much as he wanted to see her, there was a plus to Simone not knowing he was already back from his supposed trip to Ireland.

He kicked the engine into gear and reversed off the driveway, carrying on past the cottage down the dirt trail for about a mile. Luckily, no other cars came by, as there were no lay-bys on the track to pull over and let people pass. A substantial, albeit run-down, shed appeared, and he pulled off the track, parking behind the shed where nobody could see his car from the road. He could wait for Simone from there without her knowing or thinking he was being over the top. He never wanted to be too far away if she needed him, so he would do whatever it took to keep her safe.

Simone

There was no place more perfect than a strong shower for gathering Simone's thoughts. The harshness of a powerful jet could wash away stress and bad memories, as well as dirt. She'd known the cottage was perfect as soon as she'd seen how forceful the shower was. Or she'd *thought* the cottage was perfect until finding out it was the lair of a serial killer.

Watching documentaries and reading books about psychos was one thing; being in a serial killer's house was another altogether.

She closed her eyes and turned to the water, allowing the hot stream to run over her face whilst instrumental music played out from her phone. The melody was a live recording and echoed off the tiles as if the musician were in the room.

Even with such a beautiful distraction vying for her attention, the menacing note with its ominous black message played on her mind. The image of the paper was imprinted onto her brain, and it danced around inside, taunting her. Its ugly, solid handwriting wasn't familiar. The letters were blocky, as if the writer was purposefully writing differently. They were playing mind games with her. God knows why, but the why didn't really matter. The real problem was what to do about it.

An idea came to her, and she turned off the shower with a grin. The shower made her feel a little more human, though still shaky, and she switched off the music. She was careful not to burn her finger on the radiator rung as she pulled the red towel from its rail. She'd learned on day one that the radiators in the cottage always got ridiculously hot.

The warmth of the soft towel felt good against her wet skin. It reminded her of one of those hot face towels the spa used when she'd last had a facial. She hugged it tightly around her body and vaguely wondered when the last time she had a facial was. Definitely at least a year ago.

She walked into the bedroom still grinning. She was going to put her plan into action as soon as she dressed. Once dry, she pulled on a woolly, lemon-coloured jumper and some loose jeans, and sat on the bed with her phone in hand. She pulled a small business card out of her handbag, slipped her glasses back on and dialled the number printed upon it.

"DI Swanson," a man answered with an authoritative, deep voice.

Simone jumped despite being the one to call. Why did the police still make her so damn nervy after eighteen years? She almost hung up, but held her nerve.

"Hi, DI Swanson. It's Simone Johnson." She held her breath, silently praying he remembered her straight away so she wouldn't have to explain the attack.

He paused. "Hello, Miss Johnson. How are you doing?" There was a rummaging in the background as if he was looking through a drawer or desk.

"I've been OK, thank you, but I wanted to talk to you about something. If you don't mind?"

"Please do," DI Swanson replied.

She felt a wave of relief that he hadn't instantly dismissed her, though that now meant she had to tell him about her situation.

"It's a little strange. I decided to rent a cottage in the Peak District for a while – just to have a break – and I think it's possible that he's followed me here."

There was another pause and more rummaging before DI Swanson replied. "Who has followed you there?"

"The man who attacked me." She almost winced at how ridiculous she sounded. The wine was definitely getting opened later.

"You've seen him?" DI Swanson suddenly sounded far more alert.

"Well, I saw *something* just outside the boundary of the back garden, more of a shadow really, but it disappeared when I ran inside and looked again from the window. And someone tore my bike tire, too. Like completely shredded it, so I have no way of getting anywhere."

"OK. I'd like to come and chat with you in person and look around, if that's OK?"

"Yes, please do. I'd really appreciate it." Simone sighed and put her head in her hands. Thank god he hadn't struck her off as crazy.

She spent the next hour drying her hair and making sure she looked presentable, and not crazy in any way. DI Swanson had to believe her, and he wouldn't if she came across as a sleep-deprived maniac. But one glance in the mirror showed her how much she'd paled over the last few days. She applied a small amount of foundation and some mascara and checked her reflection again. She looked a little healthier. Not much, but it would have to do.

True to his word, DI Swanson was knocking on her door just

over an hour later. She glanced out of the bedroom window. He was young for a senior cop; not that much older than her. But she liked him. He was a big, protective lumberjack type. She'd trusted DI Swanson to be a man who did the right thing from the second she met him, which was rare for her. He would have been useful after her dad was murdered, seeing as those idiots hadn't believed her eyewitness account, and the murderer was never convicted. She rushed down the corridor to open up the front door.

"Hi." She grinned awkwardly at him before remembering scared people didn't grin. She looked away quickly and cleared her throat, forcing her face into more of a concerned grimace before looking back at him.

"Hello, Simone." DI Swanson gave her a short, awkward smile, as if it wasn't something he did often.

"Please, come in." She waved him into the corridor, and the pair made their way to the kitchen. "I hope the drive wasn't too bad?"

"No. The drive was fine, thank you. It was quicker than I expected."

"Oh, that's good. Take a seat." Simone motioned to the dining table. "Would you like a drink?"

"Water would be great, thank you," he replied, taking a seat at the head of the dining table.

"Sure." She stepped to the cupboard to grab a pint glass. Her stomach lurched as she remembered necking the wine the previous night.

"So, do you want to tell me more about your concerns?" he asked as she busied herself with pouring a glass of water. He was getting straight to the point, as usual.

Simone opened the freezer to find some ice. "OK. It might

sound a little strange, but two days ago I freaked out because I saw someone standing at the back door. When I took a closer look through the window, it turned out to be a man called Tom Raddish. He's the maintenance guy. The same evening, I fell asleep on the sofa and woke to a hunting knife on the table—"

"A knife?" DI Swanson looked concerned.

"Yes. It was the same one used in the attack." The glass clinked as Simone threw a couple of ice cubes into his water.

"Why didn't you call me then?"

She crossed the kitchen to put the glass down on the table in front of him and saw his eyes glance over at the empty wine bottles on the side of the counter. Damn it. They should have gone straight in the bin.

"Well, my boyfriend turned up, and he said he saw it in the kitchen when we arrived. He'd used it at some point. He thought I'd probably used it too without realising and just left it there. And I believed him. Or convinced myself I believed him, at least. He's a therapist, you see. He's very level-headed and helps me a lot." She paused, wondering if she was talking too much about Theo.

"OK." He nodded for her to continue and took his first sip of water.

"And then yesterday, I went to get my bike out of the shed at the front, and someone had slashed it."

"Slashed?"

Simone nodded. "That's what it looked like. A huge tear, which was far too big to be an accident."

"And why didn't you call the police at that time?"

"Well, again my boyfriend came round. He said it looked more like an animal had done it. Maybe a rat with big teeth, or it might have gotten stuck on a nail as I pulled it out."

DI Swanson shifted in his chair. "Hmm, and where's your boyfriend now? Can I speak to him?"

"Oh, he's in Ireland visiting family. He should be back soon."

"Do you mind me asking how long you guys have been together, Simone? I don't remember you mentioning a boyfriend previously."

"A few months. We actually met not long after what happened."

He cocked his head. "And how did you meet?"

Simone hesitated, but surely DI Swanson wouldn't care. It was hardly his department to shop therapists who fall for their clients. "Well, I first went to him for therapy. He has his own practice in Derby. But nothing happened until I was no longer a client of his."

"How nice. What's his name?"

"Theo Beckly. He's a great guy. He really looks after me." She beamed at DI Swanson.

"It would be good to speak to him when he's back. If you can, please have him call me. In the meantime, I'll look around the area and see if the local police can patrol around here for you."

"Oh, thank you. That would be fantastic."

"And if anything else happens, do let me know. But call the local police first or 999 if needed. They can get here quicker than me, and it's important that you're safe."

She showed him outside, and he nodded to her before walking off through the woodland. Simone's tense shoulders dropped. She knew she could trust DI Swanson to listen. If anyone was hiding out in the woods, he would find them. And he would believe her word over theirs.

Theo

Theo cursed as he tripped over a root peeking up from the soft woodland ground. He put his hand out to the thick tree in front of him to save his fall and landed heavily against the trunk. He cursed again and bent down to rub the pain away from his twisted ankle. Despite knowing these parts like the back of his hand, one thing he loved the most about the woodland moors and hills of the Peak District was the way they changed. Not just over the years, but season to season, each spot looked completely different.

The sound of rustling made his head snap back up. He froze, listening intently to the unmistakable sound of footsteps through the undergrowth. They came from a few hundred yards to his right, but when he turned to get a better look, the sun shone in his eyes and obstructed any proper view. He stepped back and flattened himself against the tree.

The footsteps thudded closer. And then stopped.

Theo held his breath, not daring to make a noise. What if it was Simone? And she caught him sneaking around when he'd told her he was in Ireland? He couldn't bear the thought of losing her trust now after all of his hard work. But they sounded too heavy to be Simone. If it wasn't her, though, who the hell was sneaking around her cottage? Maybe it was that bloody maintenance guy, Tom.

Curiosity beat his panic, and he slowly turned his body to peek around the trunk. A large man stood there in a black suit, facing the opposite direction. Why on earth would a man in a suit be walking through the woods? Could it be the police?

He certainly had that authoritarian confidence about him he'd seen in police officers before. The man took one last look to his left and walked away towards the cottage.

A stab of jealousy hit Theo in the gut. He had to find out for sure who this guy was and why Simone had another man around whilst she thought Theo was in a different country.

He inched his way forward and followed the same path the stranger walked. It was a straight path back to the cottage, so Theo could stay well back without losing him. The man stopped and looked around the woods every couple of minutes, clearly searching for something.

Or someone.

When the stranger reached the edge of the woods next to the cottage's driveway, he hopped over and walked straight up to the front door and knocked three times. The hair on the back of Theo's neck raised. This guy needed to stay the hell away from Simone. His eyes searched the surrounding ground. A heavy rock lay next to the mossy tree trunk. It had one jagged edge, which he ran his finger over. It was surprisingly sharp. He picked it up and held it steady in two hands.

Simone opened the door, looking as beautiful as ever in a simple jeans and jumper combo. A need to touch her almost overtook him, but he swallowed it down. There was no way she could see him appear from the woods. Not unless this idiot in a suit turned out to be dangerous. Though she'd nearly spotted him watching her in the garden yesterday thanks to a bloody bird.

"Hi, Officer Swanson." She smiled at the man, and jealousy stabbed Theo's stomach.

So, the man *was* from the police department. The name Swanson rang a bell somewhere in Theo's brain. Simone had mentioned him before. Maybe he was looking into the man who attacked her.

"I just wanted to let you know I've searched the surrounding area and couldn't see anything suspicious. So, like I said, I'll speak to the local team and see if they can drive around here a couple of times just to keep an eye out."

Theo gripped the rock tighter at the sound of his voice. It made his skin crawl.

"That would be great. Thank you so much." Simone's sweet voice was harder to hear than Swanson's from behind the trunk.

"No problem, I'll get a number for you to call, too. Obviously, you have mine, but I live quite far away so it would be good for you to have a local number for someone who is aware of your situation. Then you can feel safer."

Anger flared within Theo. It was his job to keep Simone safe, not this idiot. Yet Simone nodded and smiled again at DI Swanson. What made her think she needed his help?

"In the meantime, please have your new partner contact me when he arrives home. It would be great to speak to him about the things you mentioned."

"Of course. I'll ask him to call as soon as he's back."

Things? What things had she mentioned? What did she know? Theo placed the rock back on the floor and stepped backwards shakily. He had to get away before Simone saw him, or she'd never speak to him again. She already sounded suspicious if she was giving his name to the police. Did she really trust this Swanson guy more than him? Surely not.

He turned silently and crept back down the path, breaking into a jog when he was too far away to be heard. As much as he wanted to be near her, it was too dangerous with Swanson around. He'd go home, gather his thoughts, and make a plan. One that made Simone realise she didn't need anyone other than him to take care of her. Not even that crazy bitch in the hospital she spoke to every week. It would be him and her alone together, forever.

Simone

Simone locked the door behind DI Swanson and leant against it with a heavy sigh. So, as far as he was concerned, there was no one watching her in the woods. It was paranoia. But one thing she'd left out was the note someone pushed through the door calling her a liar. That wasn't something she wanted Swanson asking questions about.

Where was that person now?

She hadn't mentioned Walter Smidtts to DI Swanson, either. She'd surely sound crazy, and he was already eying up her empty wine bottles and making assumptions about her drinking habits.

She walked past the ugly antlers on the corridor wall to the kitchen and flicked on the kettle. As it boiled, she pulled the crumpled note out from her jeans pocket and gently unfolded it. It didn't say Simone on it. Maybe it wasn't even for her. Maybe it was for the owner of the house. The writer might not realise Walter Smidtts was locked away. But then she had lied about the stab wound.

And the note was hand delivered, so surely they would have seen her, and not Smidtts. But only a few people knew she was staying at the holiday home. Obviously, Theo knew, and she'd told Kerry herself. Kerry had given the address to the hospital staff, but Simone didn't know anyone who worked there.

The owners of the house knew, but who was that now Smidtts was no longer here? What did Tom Raddish call the owner? Miss something, but Simone hadn't been listening. She'd have to keep an eye out for Tom in the garden. He seemed the type to have lived in the area all his life and know everyone and everything about it.

She shoved the note back in her pocket and poured a strong cup of tea with plenty of sugar. Bringing it into the living room with her, she opened up the laptop and googled Peak District holidays on Pickford Lane and scrolled through *BnBnow*, *PeakDistrictStays* and *LodgesAway*. Not one mentioned her little cottage on Pickford Lane. She sat back and sipped her tea. Even if it was fully booked, it should surely show as an option on the website until she selected dates, unless it wasn't on the sites at all.

Theo would know. She sent him a quick text asking who he booked the house through. But the uncomfortable feeling caused by not being able to find it online stuck with her. A feeling of not knowing an important detail, or of being in the dark. She couldn't quite put her finger on it, but she didn't feel safe.

She grabbed her phone to call Kerry, then thought better of it and put the phone back down. Kerry would worry if she knew what was going on, and she needed to focus on getting better herself right now. Simone wasn't about to hold her progress back because of her own selfish problems.

But she wasn't calling Theo. He already thought she was nuts, and it was different now he was more than just her therapist. Their relationship had changed from him being a professional and her being a needy client, to a partnership where they were supposed to be equals. He couldn't feel like he had to save her all the time. That wouldn't do. They were equals. She wasn't dependent on anyone before the attack, and she refused to act like it now.

There was only one other person she could think of to ask for more information. *Walter Smidtts.* Her stomach turned at the thought, but she knew he wasn't far away in Adrenna Psychiatric Hospital. It was thirty minutes in the car at most. He would know who owned the house.

And after following murderers in books and on TV for so long, excitement creeped in at the prospect of meeting him. She could even do a story on him like one of the TV journalists who visit prisons and make documentaries. That would be a dream come true. And it kills two birds with one stone without her acting like a snivelling victim around Theo.

A buzz of nervous energy tingled her skin as she googled. She brought up the Adrenna Hospital website and browsed the visitor information page. It didn't seem too difficult to get a visit as long as the patient agreed. It's not like it was a lie. She was a real journalist. And it was time to go back to work.

Theo

The drive back to Theo's flat was painfully slow. Every light changed to red, and then there was the nervous learner driver who stayed in front for most of the trip. As soon as he reached his front door, he grabbed his phone charger and plugged in his phone. He stared at the screen, willing it to charge quicker. Although it felt like an age, the phone had enough battery after a few minutes to call Simone.

"Hey," she answered quickly, much to his relief.

"Hey, how are you, babe?" Theo tried to keep his voice calm despite the questions running around in his head.

"I'm fine," she replied.

It was obvious she was lying. How could she be fine living in a *killer's* house? And if she was, then why would she have called the police?

"Are you sure? Seen anything else lately?" He silently urged her to open up to him.

She paused. "Like what?"

"I don't know. Any other people around like Tom?"

"No. Nothing like that. Did you speak to the owner, by the way?"

"Yes ... she won't allow the refund, babe. I'm sorry."

The line was silent.

"Are you there?" Theo asked.

"Yes." She sighed heavily. "That's OK, I guess. It doesn't matter. I'm feeling less jumpy now, anyway. So, who is the owner now? I couldn't find anything online."

"It's a friend of my flatmate who suggested the place and gave me the owner's phone number. I didn't know about the connection though, babe, and I don't think he did either. I couldn't find anything else online that was free for a whole month. Nowhere affordable, anyway. I'll come over as soon as I'm home, OK?"

Maybe she would tell him the truth about Swanson if they were face to face.

"Great. I have a bit of a headache, babe. I'm going to go. Speak soon."

And with that, Simone hung up without even saying 'I love you.' She never hung up without telling him that. He grabbed a beer from the fridge and flung himself down on the bed, looking at the neat piles of her belongings stacked in the corner of his room. She had to stop lying to him. What could he do to get her to trust him?

The lie about Ireland was supposed to make her rely on him *more*. Simone didn't know his mum only lived an hour from the cottage. Being alone there should have made her reliant on him, not sneaking behind his back and calling the bloody police, telling them god knows what about him. But clearly, he'd messed up. He needed to get back to her fast. He stood and walked over to the boxes full of Simone's things. Her furniture had gone to storage, but not the boxes of more personal items. Someone needed to keep a closer eye on those, and who better than him. Though he hadn't told Simone. She might think him overcautious.

He trailed his fingers over the lid of the top box. Bertie Bear's ear poked out of the corner, and he grabbed it and pulled the tatty old bear out of the box. One large hand squeezed the bear's head and the other gripped its legs. He brought the bear to his nose and sniffed deeply. It had a weird smell, a bit like old cabbage, but there was a whiff of Simone's sweetness, too.

A loud roar escaped his chest as he pulled with all his might. The force easily ripped the old bear in two.

Panting heavily, he walked into the kitchen and threw the bear inside the bin, then went back to his beer in the bedroom, feeling calmer. He could think coherently about Simone's lies. He'd just have to tell her Bertie Bear got lost in the storage unit.

The Ireland lie was also a mistake. He'd told her a real live flight time in case she double-checked online, so he would have to wait to ensure she didn't catch him out. But after this, no more lies. He would tell the truth, and so would she. She owed it to him after everything he'd done for her. Now, he just needed to wait for the right moment.

Simone

Monday morning, Simone checked the address for the fifth time before the taxi arrived. She probably should have told Theo she was going to see Smidtts. Or at least told DI Swanson about him. But there was an unknown force urging her to take matters into her own hands, and she knew Theo would talk her out of seeing him.

And DI Swanson was alright, but the police had never been much help when she actually needed them. Not as a child to convict her father's killer, and not now. She'd vowed back then she'd never trust the police to keep her safe. So, she would find out the full story herself. She'd binged crime documentaries for years. It could be her special subject on that expert game show, *Mastermind*, for god's sake. How hard could it be?

She wondered if the taxi driver would ask why she was heading to such a place. Would he wonder if she was crazy, too? It didn't matter, she supposed. Let people think what they like.

It wasn't long before she heard the soft rumbling sound of a car outside the front of the house. She took a deep breath and opened up the front door to step outside. Smiling at the taxi driver, she turned to fumble with the keys. Shaky hands made it far more difficult than usual, but eventually she got the key in the lock. She tried to appear calm, but her legs trembled as she walked over the drive. It was fine; it was from excitement, not nerves.

"Hi," she greeted the driver as she entered the back seat of the taxi.

"Alright, duck," the driver responded in a thick, Derbyshire accent, much like Tom Raddish. "Are you going to that 'ospital? Adrenna?"

She nodded. "Yes, please."

There was a picture of the driver's taxi licence at the rear of his seat. She focused on reading it as they drove off – anything to keep the *excitement* at bay. His name was Gary, and he stayed quiet as they drove along winding lanes. He glanced at her from time to time in the mirror as if he wanted to ask her something.

She pretended not to notice his glances and stared out of the window instead as field after field whizzed by. Eventually, she felt her stomach turn, and it forced her to look out of the front window. Damn car sickness. Her mum had always said she'd grow out of it, but even at thirty-three, she still suffered. But then Mum was wrong about a lot of things in life. Like how Simone would never amount to anything. Well, investigating a serial killer as a journalist would surely prove her wrong.

As she turned to face forward, she caught Gary's eye in the mirror. He turned away, looking sheepish. Why was he looking at her like that? She pulled out her phone. Maybe she should text Theo a picture of Gary's licence.

"Are you from around 'ere, love?"

His voice startled her after sitting so long in silence, though his tone was friendly. He certainly didn't seem dangerous.

Walter Smidtts *looked* quite normal, though.

"I'm from Derby. Just out here for a bit of a break."

"Oh yes, I'm usually in the city centres, either Derby or Nottingham. Thought I'd 'ave a change of scenery and work out 'ere for a bit. You see some right sights in the cities. I'm staying with my brother. It's calmer out 'ere." Gary's eyes widened, and he laughed as though he'd said something stupid. "Other than your place, of course."

"Sorry?" Simone wished he'd stayed quiet. Awkward small talk was the last thing she needed when considering what questions to ask a serial killer.

"You know, with what 'appened." He looked at her knowingly, but when he saw her blank face he added, "With the owner's son? You do know what 'e did?"

"Oh yes. I know now. I didn't when I first rented it."

"They don't advertise that part, I suppose."

"Who's they?"

"Oh, 'is mother and brother. They're not round 'ere any-more."

Her mind instantly flashed to Tom Raddish. He'd looked vaguely familiar when she first saw him. "He has a brother, too?"

"Yep. Twins. My own brother went to school with 'em. Though 'e were a couple of years above 'em."

"Oh, wow, must have been a shock when he found out what happened." Simone tried to remember Tom's face and the image of Walter Smidtts she'd seen. Surely, he wasn't this mysterious twin brother.

"Yep." Gary's face changed again. "I thought 'e must be the reason you're going to Adrenna, you know. He's in there, last I 'eard. Thought you might be related somehow."

"Oh no. No." Simone shook her head so fast her glasses almost fell off her nose. "I'm meeting a friend who works there for lunch. Definitely not going inside! I didn't know he was in there, though. That's kinda creepy, actually."

"Do you still want to go?" Gary's face dropped. "I can take you back right now if you like?"

"Er, can you drop me off somewhere near, and I'll get my friend to meet me there?"

Gary nodded as though he agreed that was a good idea. "Yep, I'll do that. I know a nice cafe only a mile away from Adrenna."

"Great, thank you."

They continued the drive in silence, for which Simone was grateful. Gary turned off the main road and down a bumpy dirt path which led to a small car park. It surprised her to see it adjoined to a fairly new-looking building, rather than the decrepit old farm building she expected.

"This is the cafe, love. Well, it's a farm, see." He pointed to a field next to the building, which contained some grazing sheep.

"This is perfect, thank you."

She exited the taxi and waved Gary off before walking back down the dirt path. There was a sign for Adrenna, which showed the hospital was located a mile further down the road. She stumbled on the grass verge beside the road, cursing that she hadn't worn trainers. Sandals were not the optimal footwear for grassy verges or dirt roads. But fifteen minutes later, she was grateful to see large turrets poking out behind the trees.

As she got closer, she saw high walls surrounded Adrenna and a wrought-iron gate. It looked more like she was heading for a prison than a hospital, which made sense considering these specific patients were probably all criminals like Smidtts. Not like poor Kerry, whose hospital was far more friendly looking. Hers was more of a large house. And the staff were ultra-welcoming. Adrenna appeared as though it would start screaming at her to get out as soon as she stepped inside, much like the Addams family house.

Even Simone had to admit her excitement was closer to terror by the time she'd reached the gate. She crept through it and followed the gravel path to the stone steps at the front of the impressive building. The architect designed it like a square U, with colossal stone turrets at each angle. The walls had grown grey over years of weathering. However, the front door was clearly a lot more recent and had barely weathered at all. There was also a brand-new-looking intercom on the wall next to the door. She held a finger to the button, and a loud buzzer rang out through the silence. She cursed and removed her finger, looking around to make sure no one was about to jump out at her and tell her off.

"How can I help?" asked the overly excited voice of a young woman.

Her friendly voice calmed the ominous feeling in the pit of Simone's stomach.

"Hi, my name is Cat Jones. I'm a journalist here to see Walter Smidtts. I called earlier."

"Oh, yes, hi, Ms Jones. One moment, please."

Another buzzer sounded, followed by a clicking noise, and Simone pushed open the front door into a bright reception area. They'd painted it a calming mixture of pale pink and white. The powerful smell of fresh paint still tarnished the air. A young woman sat behind a reception desk with an enormous smile, showing off perfectly straight teeth against tanned skin.

Black hair fell effortlessly around her shoulders as if she'd just stepped out of a salon. Simone fiddled with her own, limp hair, suddenly self-conscious, but returned the woman's smile and walked towards her.

"Hi, Cat. They're just bringing Walter down. He'll come to the visitors' room shortly, which is right through that corridor and take a right. The first door you'll see is visitor room number one and there's tea and coffee facilities in the room. Do you need a locker for your bag?"

"Er, yes, please." Simone tried to act comfortable, like she visited secure hospitals all the time. The girl hadn't even asked for ID.

Was it really that easy to visit a serial killer? All she'd done was phone and ask to book in a visit for an article. They'd called her back one hour later to agree a time, and that was that. But she'd expected a bit more security in the actual hospital.

"Here you go." The girl held out a key no bigger than a twenty-pence piece, and Simone stepped forward to take it. Her hand trembled as she awkwardly shoved her bag into the locker. She pulled out the flimsy fake ID she'd created, which stated she was a journalist.

"Do you need to see my journalist ID?" she asked.

"Oh! Silly me, probably." The young woman laughed and held her hand out for the ID. Simone passed it to her, and after a quick look, she passed it back. Simone took it and shoved it into the locker with the rest of her belongings.

As she approached the door, the receptionist pressed another buzzer, and the door clicked open. Simone walked into another freshly painted corridor and turned to her right. A wooden door with a large, black number one sign on it was in front of her. She peered through the glass panel. Nobody was in there

130

yet.

She entered the room and ignored the tea and coffee facilities on the side. The miniature packet of chocolate biscuits was tempting, but her stomach clenched and she thought better of it. There was a plastic table in the middle of the claustrophobic room with two small chairs on either side. She took a chair and moved it away from the table to sit down.

She was not getting too close to Walter Smidtts.

Footsteps echoed down the corridor and the low rumbling of male voices made her stomach clench even more. She grabbed it with her hand. All too quickly, the footsteps were right outside the door and she stared at the glass panel with wide eyes. Walter Smidtts was right outside.

Theo

Theo left work at 10:00 a.m., after cancelling all appointments for the day. He told Tia he had a headache and she sorted the rest for him. He flew through the city on his way back to the cottage and only slowed at the speed cameras, which he knew well after so long driving the same roads. Cancelling appointments was against his stringent rules usually, but whatever Simone was up to could be dangerous. And she was far more important. Even though he loved his job, his concern for her was greater. Plus, the dark-suited man would be gone.

Theo chuckled to himself aloud at the thought of the local police doing a patrol. He'd known a couple of them well as a teenager. They probably wouldn't bother going within a mile of the place and were far more bothered about people behaving themselves on walks through the hills and preventing any perceived anti-social behaviour there.

No. The local police didn't concern him. Even if they found him, he'd tell them he owned the shed. He wasn't doing anything wrong just by being in the woods. As long as Simone didn't know.

As he left the city and moved onto the busy A52 via Ashbourne Road, he contemplated what the hell Simone was up to.

She'd seen Tom in the garden and he'd probably freaked her out, but he was a harmless guy. Tom had an IQ of about fifty if he was lucky. He'd always been slow. As a kid, his nickname was Tick. Theo started it as Thick Tom because the other Tom was called Big Tom, but it was just mashed together eventually as Tick.

Then there was the knife thing, which was weird in fairness to her, and then she'd found out about Walter Smidtts living in the house. He cursed himself aloud and hit the steering wheel with his palm. He should have told her about Smidtts and let her make her own mind up about staying there. She still might have said yes, knowing it was the only place free for a month in spring time. At least she'd have been prepared.

He turned onto the A623 through the small village of Sparrowpit and onto Mam Tor. Pretty cottages whizzed by, and he swallowed down his guilt over his lies. He imagined him and Simone living together in one of the cottages, and a little boy nearby calling him Daddy. If he lost that chance over a simple lie, then he would never forgive himself. *He* already hated himself for lying, and if he lost her, he could no longer keep her safe.

He finally reached Edale, and continued through the village and straight past the cottage, further down the dirt trail once again. The parking spot was another reason for picking the cottage. It lay right at the edge of the woods and was part of an ancient disused farm. Perfect for keeping a watchful eye on Simone. He could be there for her even when she didn't think he was around. Sometimes, even now, after all the time they'd spent together, she lied to him. This was the best way to keep an eye on her at times.

The farm was long gone. The owners had sold the bottom

edge of land off when Theo was a kid. The buyer had done nothing with it, so nobody noticed Theo's car as he pulled up behind the shed. He locked the car and turned towards the woods. The gnarled trees were ancient, and some stretched to six metres in height. Clouds hid the sun and a cool breeze washed over his bare arms. He regretted being in too much of a rush to grab a jacket, but he shook off the cold and began the mile-long walk back to the cottage. He took his time, more cautious than usual thanks to DI Swanson and the tiny possibility of the local police running a patrol.

Fifteen minutes later, he reached the other side of the woods, and the short path which led to the cottage spread out in front of him. He stayed well back, just watching the building at first. He peered at each window. No movement came from any of them.

He snuck through the trees to the front of the house and came out near the shed where the bike lay. He peered around the shed until he could see into the living room window. There was still no movement. He pulled out his phone and tried to call Simone. It went straight to voicemail.

His hands squeezed into fists, his fingernails digging into his palms. What if she already knew what happened, and she'd told the police? She could have found out somehow. Maybe that was why Swanson was so desperate to talk to him. He shook his head. She wouldn't tell the police without talking to him first. She wouldn't just assume he was the bad guy. Why would she? And if they locked him up, he wouldn't be able to keep her safe anymore. Surely, she would see that.

He snuck around to the front of the shed and pulled open the door. Simone still hadn't locked it. It was unusually careless of her, but he was grateful for the lapse in judgement. Tiny goose pimples covered his bare arms, but stepping into the shed helped protect him from the cool breeze. He pushed some tins of paint to one side with his foot and made a space on the floor to sit down, leaving the door the tiniest bit ajar so he could keep an eye out for Simone. He didn't mind waiting for her, but when she got back, she was going to tell him the truth. Somehow, he'd make sure of it. It was time they both stopped telling lies.

Simone

The first thing Simone noticed about Smidtts was the smell. He stunk of cheap deodorant like a teenage boy going to his first high school dance, which wasn't great for her weak stomach. His bald head shone as though he'd oiled it moments ago, and he'd grown a fuzzy beard since the police caught him, which now needed a trim. He didn't dress in some sort of hospital uniform as she'd expected; instead, he wore dark tracksuit bottoms and a plain, navy T-shirt.

She didn't stand to greet him. She peered up at him from her chair, though he was much shorter than she'd imagined he would be. It was strange, really. Walter Smidtts was an evil monster. Yet even in person he looked like any other average guy in his early forties.

He gave her a crooked smile as he took a seat on the opposite side of the table, baring yellowed teeth. She instinctively smiled back and thanked god she'd had the brain capacity to move her own chair away from the table. Even still, the foot-wide distance of the measly plastic table was nowhere near enough space between them.

Her mind whirred at a million miles an hour, unsure how to react to him or what to say. She glanced over at the young support worker who stood in the open door, facing away from them. She supposed his stance was an attempt at providing security for her whilst simultaneously giving them some semblance of privacy. It was pointless, however. The guy would clearly still hear every word spoken between them.

He was a stocky bloke, though, and the sight of his thick-set arms made her feel safer in Smidtts's presence. She cleared her throat and straightened in her seat.

"Hi, Walter, I'm Cat Johnson," she said, putting on her best business voice and staring him straight in the eye.

"I know who you are, love," he replied in a soft voice, which made her upper lip curl, though she hid it quickly. "I hear you're writing a book about me?"

She shook her head. "Not a book, no. Just an article in the local paper. If you don't mind?"

He pursed his lips as if considering some sort of deal. "Well, what would you need me to do?"

She blinked hard, trying not to shudder at every word he uttered. "Just have a conversation with me, that's it."

"What about?" He narrowed his eyes and looked her up and down.

She didn't blame him for being suspicious. How many people came to see him? Did he sit alone in his room most days? Or did he get love letters from those crazy women who threw themselves at serial killers? Maybe he even got visits from them. She cleared her dry throat again.

"Oh, you know, just about you and your childhood. Where you grew up, what the house was like, a little about your family maybe—"

"Oh, you want to know about Mark?" His smile grew wider.

She paused. The name Mark didn't ring a bell from the articles she'd read. She'd have to tread carefully.

"Who's Mark?" she asked.

He sniggered at her question. "Who's Mark? He's the bad one, of course."

Oh no. This guy really was mentally ill. Her heart sank. She wouldn't get much sense out of him if he was just babbling about made-up bad people.

"The bad what?" she asked.

He looked her up and down again, but much slower this time. His eyes took in every inch of her. She somehow fought the urge to get up and run, and stayed completely still. There was no way he was having the satisfaction of getting to her. He was clearly trying to gauge her before answering her questions.

Or was he thinking about bashing her skull in like he did the other women?

"He's my … friend. He made me do some bad things in the past."

There was that voice again, almost childlike. A part of her wished he'd refused to answer, so she didn't have to hear him speak again. She crossed her legs and sat back in her chair.

"I've read quite a bit about you, but I haven't heard of Mark before."

"Mark is the bad one," he repeated. His smile disappeared, his mouth now set in a stubborn line as if challenging her to call him a liar.

Out of the corner of her eye, she noted the support worker turn to face them. She glanced over. He rolled his eyes at her and turned away again. She pulled her attention back to Smidtts.

"I see," Simone said slowly, buying time while she tried to mash the random trains of thought into one tangible sentence. "So, you wouldn't have done those … *things* without the

138

influence of Mark?"

"Nope. Ask Gabriella. She will tell you," he replied in full confidence.

Oh great, another name she didn't recognise. This was not going how she'd planned. "Who's Gabriella?"

"You don't know much for someone who wants to write an article about me." He gave a dramatic sigh. "Mark tried to kill Gabriella. She survived. She told the police it wasn't me, but they didn't believe her, or they thought they knew better or something."

Simone wracked her brain. Surely a survivor would have been mentioned in articles somewhere, but that wasn't a detail she'd have forgotten. "A survivor? I heard nothing about any survivor."

"Gabriella Beaufort. The police didn't widely share the information because she tells everyone it wasn't me who tried to kill her. Nobody needed to know a bad guy was still out there."

A sharp ache ran through the top of Simone's head, and she put her hand up to ease the pain. "OK. You've been very helpful, thank you."

"Are you OK?" Smidtts asked her. He leant forward in his chair, looking genuinely concerned. Wow, the guy could act.

"I actually don't feel great. I am sorry. We might have to cut this meeting short." Simone stood. Smidtts sat back in his chair. She'd expected him to be angry, but he was still calm as anything. "Actually, one last question. What happened to the house they arrested you in?"

"Nothing. It's not mine. It was my mother's and still is. Do you want to set up another meeting?" he asked, his face etched in hope.

"Yes, definitely. I'll call soon and give you some dates, OK?"

Simone gave him a wide berth as she walked towards the door. The support worker moved out of her way and stepped over to Smidtts. The white badge on his shirt read *Harrison* in bold, black letters.

"I'll be back for you in a minute, Walter," said Harrison, and he turned to follow Simone into the hall and back to the reception area.

"Mark is his imaginary friend, by the way. We hear him talking to him sometimes in his room," he said as Simone walked through the door. "Hey, can I be in your article? Anonymously, of course. I know everything about him." He gave her a wide smile, as if trying to impress her.

"Er, sure. Maybe. I'll call you."

"Great! My name is Harrison Woods, if you want to write it down."

She nodded. "Will do."

He beamed and closed the door behind her. An urge for fresh air hit her, and she rushed to the locker to grab her things.

"Good visit?" the spirited receptionist asked.

"Yes, fine, thanks," Simone automatically responded as she grabbed the register from the counter and signed out. She almost wrote her own name and had to scribble it into Cat quickly before the receptionist noticed.

Thoughts raced through her mind as she left the hospital and walked down to the cafe to order another taxi back. So, Walter denied being the only one who hurt those women. He was insistent there was someone else out there. And Simone agreed. That same person was likely the one who attacked her. But to find out more, she needed more information. She needed to speak to Gabriella Beaufort.

140

Theo

Theo sat huddled on the floor of the shed, attempting to read a book on his phone, but his legs were numb and his concentration was low. The paragraphs kept jumbling into one. After re-reading one particular sentence three times, he gave up and put his phone back in his pocket.

He stretched his aching legs out and checked the time on his watch. It had been ninety minutes since he'd first shown up, and there was still no movement from the house or any sign at all of Simone. He kicked a nearby tin of paint, regretting it almost instantly as pain shot through his big toe. Ninety minutes stuck in a cold shed, just to make sure she was OK. And she'd never even know of his efforts.

He considered going home, but then the low rumbling of a car engine floated down the road. He snuck out of the shed, quick as a flash, and ducked down behind it once more. Making sure he wasn't visible, he peered around the far corner and saw a dark car in the distance. It wasn't one he recognised. His whole body tensed as it drew nearer. But as it pulled onto the drive, a 'Taxi' sign on top of the roof became visible and his body relaxed.

At least it wasn't a cop car, with that Swanson idiot at the helm looking to arrest him.

As the car got closer, he could see a man in the driver's seat and Simone in the back. She was looking down at something with a strange look on her face. He moved so he was completely behind the shed, and kept still.

The car door slammed shut, and footsteps crunched over the gravel leading to the front door. After a moment, the front door slammed shut and the car rolled away. Once he could no longer hear the engine, he risked peeking out again. There she was in the living room window. His heart soared at the sight of her. She sat down on the sofa and bent over something, a phone or a laptop, maybe. He pulled out his own phone and dialled her number, never taking his eyes off her. She lifted her head and leaned forward to pick up the phone.

"Hello," she answered.

He'd been so lost in watching her that hearing her voice on the phone threw him. He said nothing for a moment, still staring at her outline through the window.

"Theo?" she asked in a confused voice.

He watched her stand up and pace the living room.

"Yes, it's me, hi. I couldn't hear you for a moment. Are you OK?"

"Yes, I'm fine. Are you OK? You sound weird."

"I'm just trying to talk quietly. My mum's sleeping. But good news, I can get an earlier flight. They've had a cancellation. I'll be back tonight."

"Oh, that's great!"

He watched her sit back down on the sofa and twiddle her hair. She always played with her hair when nervous. Why would she be nervous about seeing him?

"I can't wait to see you. I hope you haven't been too bored without me?" he asked.

She chuckled softly. "I've just been chilling at the cottage, really."

More lies. "You haven't been out anywhere?" He struggled to keep his voice level.

"Nope. Nowhere to go." She chuckled again.

He bit his tongue hard. "Well, I'll be back soon and we can have some fun together. Maybe I'll take you out for a meal?"

"Sounds great. I can't wait to see you, babe."

At least she sounded sincere about seeing him.

"Love you," he whispered.

"Love you, too."

The line went dead and Theo slowly put the phone down, not taking his eyes off Simone. She hadn't even asked him what time he'd be back, or if he was coming to see her. He needed to know what she knew. He needed to find out everything that was online about Walter Smidtts. Something about her research had made her act off with him, and he was going to find out what. It was time to stop watching Simone and do his own research back home.

Simone

Back in the kitchen on Monday evening, Simone tentatively pulled out a bottle of white wine from the fridge. The tight feeling in her stomach had lessened knowing that Smidtts was definitely locked up. He wasn't watching her or creeping into the woods, and his mum still owned the house. She'd clearly been unable to stay there after the arrest and simply rented it out. Nothing too strange about that. It's not like they ever found any bodies near the cottage. They were all in the city. But that meant someone *else* was watching the house, or had at least seen Simone. The same someone who had left that note, which she could only assume was for her and not for Walter.

She sighed and poured herself a large glass of the ice cold Chilean Sauvignon Blanc. Not that she knew much about wines, but Kerry had once told her during a shopping trip that the Chilean brand was the nicest. From then on, Simone only purchased that same brand wherever possible. She stared at the glass for a moment, knowing it was a bad idea. But brought it to her lips regardless and took a sip, making a promise to herself that she wouldn't drink any more after tonight. Her eyes closed, and she smiled. The taste brought with it memories of Kerry's laughter and their meals out, summer BBQs and concert trips.

Kerry would know what to do if she were here.

She trudged through the corridor to the living room with her glass and sunk into the sofa, feeling exhausted. The temptation to close her eyes was strong, but she forced them open and popped the glass on the coffee table while she set up the laptop on her knee. Then she grabbed the wine again and continued to sip.

She logged into her dormant social media accounts. It had been at least a year since she'd last posted on any of them. Since Kerry had stopped tagging her in things, she hadn't made a post. She resisted the urge to look through old photos in her reminiscent mood and opened the search bar instead, typing in Gabriella Beaufort's name and hitting enter.

She grinned when she saw the results. She got lucky. There was only one Gabriella Beaufort living in Derbyshire.

"Hello," Simone muttered as she clicked on Gabriella's profile and sipped more of her wine.

Gabriella stared out from her profile picture. Her dark eyes stood against pale skin. They matched her deep-brown, shoulder-length hair. Simone felt a tightness in her chest. Maybe she should leave this woman alone. She scrolled past the profile picture hoping to find some more information about the mysterious-looking woman, but Gabriella had locked the profile down other than the previous profile pictures. The woman stood on top of a hill in the Peak District in one photo. She looked away from the camera and out into the view of the rolling hillsides. In another, she had a cocktail in her hand and was in the middle of two friends, smiling. She looked happier and less intimidating.

Fuck it.

Simone hit the message option and took one last sip of Dutch courage before she plonked the glass back on the coffee table. She spilt some of the wine as the glass hit the table.

"Oops!" She chuckled out loud. It had gone straight to her head thanks to an empty stomach and too many quick sips. She flexed her fingers as she considered what to say to this stranger who made her chest tight just from a picture. She typed *'Hey'* and then deleted it. Then *'Hi,'* and deleted that too. But eventually, after a few more tries, she settled on a casual message.

'Hey, sorry to message you out of the blue. I was hoping to speak to you – I'm a fellow survivor.'

That should do it. She sounded friendly, but the message insinuated a common bond through a shared experience – no details or explicitness. And hopefully no trigger words which would upset Gabriella.

She closed the laptop down and lay back on the sofa. She needed something to take her mind off Gabriella whilst she waited for a response. There was no point checking her messages every two minutes all night. Either Gabriella would reply or she wouldn't. Stressing out about it wouldn't help, and the wine helped with that.

She flicked on the TV for some background noise and chose another light-hearted chick flick to watch. God knows she needed a laugh after the last twenty-four hours. Her eyes flicked over to the window, which took up most of the front wall of the living room. The sky was turning dark, and she still had enough wits about her to realise she needed to get up and close the curtains.

She groaned and hauled herself up to close the curtains, and made the effort to double-check the front and back doors were locked before settling back down on the sofa again. The comfortable double bed looked inviting as she passed the room, but there was no way she was sleeping in there. The sofa felt less dangerous somehow.

She sank into the soft cushions of the sofa, grateful to rest her heavy head and tired eyes, though her mind continued to swirl through a million different thoughts. She tried to push through the mist to focus on the note. She needed to be certain about who left it.

The person clearly didn't want to break in and attack her, or they would have done it. There'd be no warning signs or notes left. Maybe they just wanted her to confess. Or were they expecting to blackmail her somehow? Though she had no money, so what could they possibly want in return? Her thoughts slowed as the tiredness won. But she remembered one final thought. They wanted to scare her. They wanted to make her worry and panic and fall apart. But she wouldn't give them that satisfaction. She was stronger than they realised, and she wouldn't let them win.

Theo

B ack at his flat, Theo settled into the uncomfortable sofa as best he could with another cheap beer in hand. Sitting on the homey sofa of the cottage would be far better, with Simone safe in his arms and the sweet smell of her hair filling his nose. He straightened a coaster on the table and removed his ring, fiddling with it in his other hand.

There was no point hanging around to watch Simone all night if she didn't want him there. So, he'd text and said he was too tired to visit tonight after the flight. It didn't seem to bother her one bit. Sneaking around outside was too much hard work if she wasn't appreciative of his efforts. Cameras would be a better option in the future. Though, they would have to be small ones.

Anyway, if he wanted her to open up to him, he first needed to know what she'd found out about Smidtts that had spooked her so much. It was baffling that she didn't yet realise she could tell him anything, and he'd still love the bones of her. He was a therapist, for Christ's sake. He heard weird thoughts from strangers all day long. And yet here he was, having to sneak around and research what she was looking at just to help her. He hit play on the *Murder Me Wrote* podcast episode.

He rolled his eyes as soon as the podcast started and fought the urge to turn it off. The young presenter sounded like he was telling a ghost story to a small child rather than discussing a real-life serial killer. He was probably one of those attention-seeking, social media-obsessed influencers. Theo took a swig of the bitter beer and hoped it would help his concentration.

'*Get ready for a true horror story folks, because Walter Smidtts was a killer like no other I've seen. Unlike most serial killers, Smidtts took the time to stalk his victims. He meticulously chose young, white women with long brown hair and got to know them. First, he learned their routines from a distance. Then, when he knew what times they'd be alone, he followed them and jumped out at them on the street. He beat them until they were unconscious and then stole their clothes and bags and abandoned them, naked and hurt and terrified. The women thought this was the end of their ordeal and that they'd escaped with their lives, but they were wrong. Smidtts was just getting started.*'

Theo hit pause and gulped down the rest of his beer, not sure how much more of the dramatic flair he could take from the podcaster. He placed his ring back on his finger, stretched, and walked over to the kitchen to place the empty bottle into the recycling container, standing it neatly next to the other bottles. He thought about Simone being alone in the cottage and stuck in a dark whirlwind of thoughts. She'd probably struggle to sleep without him. But maybe that's what she needed in order to see he was perfect for her. It wasn't a punishment to leave her alone – more an encouragement to make her appreciate him. He grabbed another beer from the fridge before returning to the sofa and hitting play.

'*Smidtts would continue to stalk the girls, pretending to be their friend and helping them through their ordeal. But thirty days later, he would kidnap, torture and kill them. This is the story of how he did it, and how he got away with it for well over a year.'*

Pfft. It was a lot longer than a year. Theo hit pause again. Why was Simone so obsessed with this guy? She knew he was locked away. She couldn't think he had anything to do with what happened to her. Or that he was coming back to get her. The police caught him two years ago. Which was way before anyone attacked her. Maybe being in his house was causing her to have obsessive thoughts.

Maybe he needed to medicate her. It might be the only way she'd rest and listen to him. She'd stop running around and sneaking behind his back. Medication would force her to rest and heal. It would be good for her. Though he'd need to be around her a lot to keep up the dosage.

She could stay in his flat. He grinned at the thought of her being in his arms in the flat. He'd never have to miss her again. She'd be waiting for him to return from work each day. He could sink into her whenever he wanted, in whichever way he wanted. All he had to do was convince her to move in with him. It would be temporary at first, of course. That way she might say yes. And then he'd make sure she'd never want to leave by making sure she had plenty of rest and giving her anything she wanted. Smidtts would be nothing but a distant memory, and so would that crazy bitch, Kerry.

Simone

Simone awoke on the sofa to a throbbing head and her tongue stuck to the roof of her mouth. Ugh. Whatever was left over from that cheap bottle of wine really had to go in the bin. The hard wood of the sofa arm dug into her shoulder, and she rolled onto her side with a groan. She opened one eye and the blurry living room came into view.

She blinked hard a few times to clear her vision as she tried to remember the misty events of the night before. A creeping anxiety was rolling around in her stomach. She'd done something, but what? The TV was off. Nothing was out of place. Her laptop was yards away on the floor. Her eyes locked on her phone, sitting innocently on the floor.

Gabriella Beaufort.

The anxiety wrestled with her stomach, and she shot off the sofa to dive for her phone. She prayed she'd only sent a simple message, and a wave of relief tranquilised her stomach as she saw her message was friendly and clean. There was no response. Maybe that was a good thing. Maybe she just needed to chill out about this whole thing, go to a B&B and get a credit card or something to pay the costs. She laid her phone on the coffee table and rubbed her face.

What on earth was she doing texting a survivor of a serial

killer? Opening up Gabriella's wounds for no reason other than her own paranoia that someone was watching her? Or was it some silly feeling that she'd ended up in Smidtts's home for a reason? A feeling that she was supposed to do something. That there was something for her to investigate. It was surely just the journalist talking, but she was never usually wrong about her feelings. As she looked up, her stomach turned inside out once again.

Gabriella Beaufort is typing...

Oh, god. She put her head back in her hands. If only she could delete the damn message.

Maybe she'd just tell Simone to go away. That would be the best outcome. Then she could get back to her B&B fantasy and get away from all of this weird Smidtts stuff, and never, ever tell Theo. Though he probably wouldn't get mad. He'd never lost his temper around her. It was strange, really. Everyone had a boiling point. Maybe her sneaking around chatting to serial killers would be his. Hopefully she wouldn't find out, because he'd never know as long as she stopped acting so crazy.

She raised her head again, one eye open, and looked at the phone. Gabriella was still typing. It was a long message, whatever she was trying to say. She probably couldn't decide what to say. Or maybe it was a long rant about how ridiculous it is to contact a survivor of a known serial killer. Especially by saying she was a fellow survivor. Now Simone would have to explain that she didn't mean she was a survivor of Smidtts, but of a different random attack. How stupid would that make her sound?

She stood and stretched her body in a feeble attempt to release some of the tension. The ache in her head intensified, so she grabbed her phone and stumbled to the kitchen to get some water. She threw the phone onto the counter as she drank, and it skidded the screen down on the wooden side. She shrugged, not caring much if it broke. Though then she'd be stuck here with no phone and no car. She twisted the phone over in a panic. But it was fine.

And Gabriella was still typing.

She peered out of the blinds, looking into the back garden. It was still. Even the birds didn't seem to be awake, or something had scared them away. She stepped closer to the window so she could view the garden in full and craned her neck to look to the left. And then she saw him.

A man stood near the gate with his back to her. He was bending over a wheelbarrow. He must have felt her staring at him, because he turned at that moment and grinned widely, one hand up in a wave. She smiled and waved back, one hand on her stomach to stop the bile that had risen when she spotted him.

If the owner wouldn't let her leave early with a refund, maybe she could make Tom stay away. It was too nervy being in this house as it was without a strange man turning up at all hours of the day doing whatever it was he did. She could do without a gardener for a month, surely. She sighed and sat down at the kitchen table, still sipping her glass of water. What a day, and it was only 9:00 a.m.

Her eyes flicked over to the phone, still on the kitchen counter where it had landed. As if it felt her anxiety-fuelled stare, it vibrated.

A message alert.

She didn't move at first, unsure if she could handle what the message said. If she ignored it, she wouldn't have to do anything. Well, other than getting out of this godforsaken cottage. But curiosity won, and she scraped the chair across the floor and stood determinedly, marching over to the kitchen side to grab the phone. She stared at the locked screen for a moment.

One new message from Gabriella Beaufort.

OK. Breathe. Time to open it.

She unlocked the phone with bated breath and clicked on the message icon.

'Hi Simone, how can I help?'

Simone stared at the response. It was a significant question. How could Gabriella help her? What good would it do to speak to her? It was time to admit what had been bugging her all along. If Smidtts was right and he did not attack Gabriella, then a helper of the Lunar Killer was loose. And he might be the same man who attacked Simone. Despite her fears, it was worth a chat with Gabriella.

'Hi Gabriella, I was hoping we could meet up?'

It was a question worth asking, but she couldn't ask it over a message. Luckily, she didn't have to wait as long for a response this time.

'Sure, when and where?'

Theo

Darkness swirled around Theo as he slept. Repugnant shadows of women with rotten corpses reached out with animal-like claws longer than his arms. The rancid smell of decomposed flesh clogged his nose to the point he could barely breathe. The smell snuck into his throat and he tasted the festering meat.

He tried to sit up, to get out of bed, to run away, anything to get away from the shadows. But they gripped his body with an invisible force and held him down in the bed. His head sunk deep into the sudden mountain of pillows underneath him. They were no longer his own fresh pillows, but ones yellowed with sweat and covered in bits of flesh dropped from the shadows. Yet they were so soft his head fell right through them, and the fabric covered his mouth making it harder and harder to breathe. He tried to scream, but no noise came out, and just as he was about to take a final, strangled breath, he awoke to more darkness and a heavy fabric on his face.

He flung the duvet off his body and daylight penetrated the pale-blue walls of his bedroom. Rotten corpses were nowhere to be seen. Sweat soaked his body and sheets, and he sucked in deep breaths. He stared at the window next to his bed. The daylight through the blinds flooded him with relief. It was fine.

Just a nightmare. There was nothing to fear.

He breathed in the fresh air from the open window, filling his lungs as deeply as he could with the smell of petrol fumes, pubs, and takeaways. The unpleasant smell of inner-city life. He'd never enjoyed it so much as he did at that moment. He scrambled off the bed, eyeing the pillows warily as he went.

He opened up the blinds to let the light flood the room further and checked the time on his phone. It was 10:00 a.m. Wow, he never slept this late. Especially on a weekday, and it was only Tuesday. He tried to remember what time he'd gone to bed after listening to that stupid podcast. It was quite late, and a fair number of beers had been the only way to get through it. He wouldn't be listening again if it caused nightmares as real as that one.

He shuddered and turned to rush into the tiny en suite shower room. Despite breathing in the morning air of the city, he still felt the smell clogging up his lungs. The image of rotten flesh was stamped onto his eyelids whenever he blinked. He had to climb over a lot of Simone's things to get to the en suite.

He switched on the shower and threw his pants to one side, jumping in before the water had a chance to heat up. But the shock of the cold water on his face forced away the remnants of terror from the dream and cleared his lungs of the smell. The water warmed, and his body relaxed.

But now this whole business with Smidtts was also messing with *his* head, and it needed to stop. He wondered what Simone was doing. He missed the feel of her smooth skin and the softness of her voice. Did she miss him? She hadn't called last night.

As soon as he was out of the shower, he grabbed his phone

and sent her a text to say he'd be over tonight. There was no way he wanted another nightmare like the one he'd just had. One way or another, he had to sort this mess today, starting with ending Simone's obsession.

He ran his finger along the edge of one of the cardboard boxes that stored Simone's possessions. He opened up the flap and rifled through the soft fabrics inside. They were mainly clothes she didn't wear much, but his thumb hit something solid and he turned his palm to grab it. His fingers clasped around a book and he pulled it out from the dark jumper it was wrapped up inside. It was her treasured copy of *Little Women*.

He opened up the book and breathed in the mouldy smell. God knows why Simone loved such things. A stab of jealousy cut through his stomach upon seeing the handwritten message inside. It simply read *'Love you, Dad'*. He opened the book to the middle and ripped out some of the pages. Not too many. It wouldn't be noticeable until she reached the middle of the story. And he gently placed the book back into the box, and wrapped the jumper around it.

Simone

Simone reread her message to Gabriella one last time and hit send, crossing her fingers for a quick reply. Within seconds, the phone buzzed again.

'The cafe would be perfect. Should get there about 1pm?'

Finally, something was going right. Gabriella had requested they meet somewhere in public and away from the city, so the farm cafe where Gary dropped her off previously fit the bill. Which was lucky, as it was the only place she knew of nearby for a chat.

She typed furiously to confirm 1:00 p.m. was OK before calling Peak District Taxis and requesting Gary to pick her up. Better not to have anyone else knowing where she was staying, if she could help it. And Gary was so harmless.

"Yes, Gary will be there at half past twelve, love," the receptionist confirmed.

Everyone was 'love' or 'duck' around here. An hour later, she allowed the last drops of water to run over her face before getting out of the shower. Gabriella mentioned she lived just outside of the city in the large town of Spondon, having moved from the city following her ordeal. So, she was likely on her way to the cafe already. Unless she was the type to be late, or she chickened out. Simone wouldn't blame her for changing her mind. If it was the other way round, she probably wouldn't have even replied to such a cryptic message.

Asking the right questions was vital, especially after having been woefully unprepared when meeting with Smidtts. That couldn't happen again. Admitting the right amount of information was important, too. Nothing about the visit with Smidtts in Adrenna. Nobody ever needed to know that and if anyone checked, they wouldn't see her name on the visitors' log. So that could stay her little secret. It wasn't like they'd ever let Smidtts out. She'd never run into him on the street whilst out and about with Theo. Smidtts would never know who she really was.

And nothing about being followed, either. Or the note. No. She'd have to be very careful about what she revealed. Simply that a man attacked her seven months ago. He'd mentioned something about 'no four weeks this time,' and Simone was concerned it was the same person who'd attacked Gabriella. That would do.

Simone wrapped the warm towel around her and dried her body, being careful around the scar on her thigh. It was still an angry red, and sensitive to touch thanks to the tearing of muscle. The doctor said it would take six to twelve months to heal completely. But the pain felt good. She didn't want it to go away. The ugly scar was a constant reminder of strength. She thumbed the scar and pushed down. It still caused enough pain to release tension – and remind her why she was meeting Gabriella.

After a few seconds, the pain became too much and she took her thumb away. She continued to pat down the rest of her body until her skin was mostly dry. The soft carpet of the hallway felt good between her bare toes. Walter Smidtts played in her mind again. Had he walked down here barefoot, too?

She shook the thoughts away and tugged out the one unpacked suitcase from under the bed. She'd unpacked most bags, but this one was full of things she hadn't thought she'd need. Smart clothes, the trinket box from her grandmother and heels. Who needed heels in the Peak District?

There was a little black dress, which was far too over the top. She could surprise Theo by wearing it one night, maybe. Two blouses and some formal black trousers were balled into the bottom of the case. There were also a couple of more revealing tops, again meant more for Theo than anything else.

She selected the black trousers and a pale-blue blouse, and checked herself out in the bedroom's full-length mirror. A bit too smart for a casual lunch in the cafe. What would Gabriella wear? The last thing she needed was for her to feel intimidated. They were survivors. Bonded by a common experience. Kindred spirits, even. And her outfit needed to reflect that.

Simone pulled up Gabriella's social media account again and scrolled through the profile pictures she could access. She dressed smartly in most of them and wore lots of simple dresses. Simone threw off the black trousers and blouse and rummaged in the wardrobe instead, settling on a knee-length summer dress and sandals with a denim jacket. She ran a brush through her hair and studied herself in the mirror, wondering if denim jackets were out of style. Fashion wasn't important, but first impressions were. It looked great with the dress, though.

She kept the jacket on and walked around the cottage to ensure every window and door was locked, and ended up back on the front drive waiting for Gary. He was a few minutes early and waved at her as he pulled into the drive. She raised a hand to say hello in return and climbed into the back of the car.

"Hi, Gary." She smiled as she pulled on the seatbelt.

"Hi, Simone innit?"

She nodded.

"Good to see you were safe after visiting Adrenna, duck."

"I was never in any danger," she replied quickly.

"Of course not." He turned the black Ford around and rolled off the drive and down Pickford Lane to head to the main road. "So, are you meeting your friend again at the cafe?"

"Yes, she's on her lunch break."

"You should definitely try their sausage. It's the best sausage in Derbyshire, for a fact. Trust me, I've driven all over, and no one has come close to beating them."

Unlike their first journey, Gary's idle chatter was comforting and calmed Simone's nerves. She still ran through her questions for Gabriella in her mind as she smiled and nodded in all the right places. She just needed to know if Smidtts had lied to her about who attacked Gabriella. As long as he was lying, then he must be the only Lunar Killer and there was no one else on the loose looking to finish her off.

Thirty minutes of idle chit chat later, they'd reached the farm and Simone peeled her eyes, looking for Gabriella. She said she drove a blue Nissan Qashqai, but there were no vehicles matching that description in the car park.

She fought an urge to run after Gary's Ford and ask him to take her home, and steeled herself to walk into the cafe alone. This was the day she would finally get answers, and she wasn't running away from that, no matter what.

Theo

Theo kept well back in his dark Insignia. He'd been following Simone for twenty minutes and the weekday roads were busier than usual thanks to Peak District ramblers wanting to get out in the sunshine while it lasted. It was unusually warm and the hot sun kept the temperature at around eighteen degrees all morning. Such crowds were usually a massive pain in the neck, but it was great to have the traffic to hide behind.

It was a good job he'd turned up at his hideout spot when he did. When he reached the woods next to the cottage at 12:20, Simone was sitting on the porch with her handbag slung over her shoulder. She'd done her makeup and dressed in a flimsy summer dress he could easily tear off her later.

He was so distracted by his thoughts that he'd barely heard the taxi appearing. But he'd seen her smile and wave as if she knew the driver. Theo had legged it back to the car, which was parked at the shed a mile long run through the woods. With it being so hot, the air was heavy in the woods and sweat still clung to him despite the air con blasting out cold air. He'd need another shower before visiting Simone that evening.

It was a prime example of why watching Simone was a good idea. He clearly wasn't the only one with a secret, and he needed to know whom she was meeting dressed the way she was. He trusted her not to cheat. She would never do that to him. But she was up to something.

Finally, the taxi pulled into some sort of farm cafe and came to a stop. Theo continued slowly down the road for a couple of minutes, pulling over in a lay-by further down. He pulled a cap over his head and wore dark sunglasses. At least the sun meant he wouldn't look out of place. As he got out, he saw the taxi driver fly by him with no Simone in the back seat.

He jogged back up the road and slowed as the cafe came into view. Simone stood in the car park, looking around as if expecting someone. Who was she expecting? Simone didn't talk to many people, preferring to keep herself to herself. She'd told him that when they first met in therapy, and he'd seen it first hand over the last few months.

He racked his brain for people she'd mentioned. But she didn't have any friends that he knew of, other than some work buddies she met with sometimes. Even that was rare, and she certainly hadn't seen any of them outside of work for a few weeks.

Then there was Kerry, who was locked away after attacking her neighbour. She'd thought he was an alien who'd come to kidnap her, or something to that effect. And she could stay locked away as far as he was concerned. From what Simone told him about some of their university fun, Kerry was not a good influence.

So, Simone only had him. She relied on him, needed him. He was the only person around to protect her, and she'd see that soon. They were meant to be.

He came across a large tree and stood behind it to watch her. She finally moved and made her way into the cafe. Was whoever she was meeting inside already?

He waited until she'd disappeared from view and then walked up the remaining road to the cafe. It wasn't one he'd been inside before, and though the farm buildings had clearly been around for a while, the cafe looked fairly new. Maybe five years old, tops. Theo wrinkled his nose.

What was worse than eating in a place that stunk of the back end of a cow? He'd rather eat fast food for the first time in sixteen years. Simone had to be more careful with what she ate at times. But at least she could cook proper food from scratch.

The car park was small but almost full, with only a few spaces left. The farmer had dotted a few benches around the edge in case people wanted to eat outside with the full stench of the cows.

Theo chose a bench behind a large people carrier so he could watch Simone through the glass window without being easily seen. It didn't look too busy inside. A few men stood at the counter and they were the only other people he could see. Simone sat alone in the middle of the cafe, thankfully close to the window. She was staring out into the car park waiting for her visitor.

A mixture of anger and jealousy pulled at Theo's chest. He turned to look out into the car park, too, but no one was around yet. When he turned back, one man inside had turned to face Simone. He was watching her, too. Theo perched further forward to squint at the man.

Tom Raddish.

Why was he staring at her like that? Goddammit. He stood up, ready to storm in and put his arm around her and tell Tom to stay the hell away.

But then he'd never know who Simone was meeting behind

164

his back.

He sat back on the bench and pulled his cap right down. Tom could wait until later. For now, he needed to know what other threats were around. And he'd only find out if he kept calm.

Simone

Simone clutched the handbag on her knees as she waited at the cafe for Gabriella. The spotty young server plonked a glass of sparkling lemonade in front of her and walked away with barely a smile in her direction. He was too busy talking to three ruddy-faced men standing at the counter to pay too much attention to her once she'd ordered. The men appeared to be regulars. They were large and jovial, and kept laughing loudly at nothing much. Simone tried to hide her irritation and focused on the car park. Luckily, there was a large window at the front of the building so she could easily see any cars coming or going.

She turned to face the window so the men's boisterous behaviour was easier to ignore, and watched through the window for a few minutes. She had to squint through the sun which beamed off the glass. Still, no one entered the car park. She sighed and checked the time on her phone. It was now quarter past one. They had agreed around 1:00-ish, so Gabriella wasn't necessarily late.

At 1:25 p.m., a blue Nissan Qashqai finally pulled into the car park. A woman with brown hair was in the driver's seat. The passenger seat next to her was empty. Phew. The last thing Simone needed was some overprotective boyfriend listening in to their conversation. Though as the car came to a stop, the woman inside didn't move. She put her head down as if she'd rather be anywhere else.

A pang of guilt pulled at Simone, but she ignored it and took a sip of lemonade as she peered at the woman. It was definitely Gabriella. She seemed to shrug herself out of her reverie and pulled down the sun visor. She fiddled around with something on the front seat and then applied some lipstick, pressing her lips together before flipping the visor back into place.

It was a relief when she finally pushed the car door open. Simone looked down quickly, picking up her phone from the table and pretending to be reading something on the screen. But she peeked up now and then to make sure Gabriella hadn't changed her mind and run back to the car.

Simone needn't have worried about Gabriella seeing her peeking. She kept her head firmly downwards as she walked through the car park. When Gabriella reached the door, Simone kept her gaze down and only looked up again once she felt a presence standing over her.

But she stared open-mouthed at the person in front of her. It wasn't Gabriella, but one of the noisy, ruddy-faced noisy regulars from the counter. It was the maintenance worker she'd found lurking in her back garden, Tom Raddish. She'd been so distracted looking out for Gabriella, she hadn't realised it was him until he was up close in front of her.

"Hello, miss," he said. His cheeks were even redder than they'd appeared in the garden. His short, curly hair shined with sweat. Or grease. Either way, it wasn't nice.

"Oh, hi. Tom, wasn't it?" She tried not to wrinkle her nose at the smell of old sweat mixed with tobacco hanging around him.

He gave a vigorous nod. He reminded her of a puppy. Daft, smelly and innocent. Had he really scared her so much? He was harmless. Everything about him screamed desperate to please rather than dangerous.

"I hope everything is OK for you up at the cottage."

"Everything is fine, thank you." She smiled up at him. "I'm actually just meeting a friend." She peered around his bulk to see where Gabriella had gone, but her heart sank. She was nowhere to be seen.

Simone jumped up out of the chair, forcing Tom to take a step back. She glanced out of the window. The blue Qashqai had disappeared.

"Sorry, Tom. I have to go. Nice to see you." Simone grabbed her jacket off the back of the chair and rushed past him.

"Let me know if you need anything, miss!" he yelled after her.

Simone ran across the car park to see if she could spot the Nissan, but it was long gone. Something had clearly spooked her.

Or *someone*.

She called the taxi firm and Gary turned up within fifteen minutes to take her home. She'd definitely need a car if she moved to the countryside. Gary cost her a bomb.

She arrived home just after 2:30 p.m., and the sun was hotter than it had been all morning. Spring was the best season. Not just because of the lighter evenings after months of darkness, but also the anticipation of summer and all that came with it. Better weather, holidays, reading in the sunshine. And best of all, Kerry might be around at last.

The growl of her stomach put a stop to her train of thought, so she locked the front door and went to the kitchen to rummage for food; ending up with a shop-bought tuna mayo sandwich she'd purchased on the same day she moved in. She rushed it down before throwing on a pair of conformable jogging bottoms and a jumper, and sitting back in the living room with her laptop.

Stomach finally quiet, she brought up another google search for Smidtts and found a site she hadn't yet read. She scrolled through the basic information about his crimes and landed on a new section which detailed how the police had found out he was behind the murders.

When Smidtts was on his killing spree, it was throughout autumn and winter three years prior, and the level of rain had been high that year. There were lots of muddy gardens and fields, and at multiple scenes they found a shoe print that was a rare Yaku, a designer brand from Italy. Though Yaku had sold hundreds in the US, they had only ever shipped five sets to the UK. More specifically, they shipped them to a small shop in the thermal spa town of Buxton, which was nestled right in the centre of the Peak District. The police found the customer details of the three people who had paid by card for their trainers, and one of them was Walter Smidtts.

The same article was the first one which mentioned Gabriella's case. This shoe print had been in the first two attacks and the final two murders. There was also DNA from some hairs which had matched Smidtts.

It certainly seemed like it was an open-and-shut case. Smidtts must have attacked Gabriella initially, because a hair was found which belonged to him. So maybe he was lying about who attempted to murder her a month later. It would hardly be surprising that a deranged serial killer would lie.

But as she scrolled down further, she sucked in a breath.

The Yaku shoe print was also found at the scene of the second attack on Gabriella.

And there was an evidence picture of the knife Smidtts had used.

It was the same knife she'd found in her living room last week. The same knife someone attacked her with seven months ago.

The phone vibrated against her thigh, and she jumped off the sofa. Her sweaty hands made pulling it out of her pocket more difficult than usual. The message was from Gabriella. She had to wipe her hands dry on her dress before the dumb screen would recognise her thumb print and open up the message, but when she finally managed, every hair on the back of her neck raised.

'Hey, sorry about today, but you're in danger. Everyone thinks Walter Smidtts tried to kill me, but that's not true. I don't know the name of the man, but he was watching you at the farm today. Please get to safety.'

Theo

The hidden stones in the soft soil dug into Theo's knees as he stooped down onto the ground. At least he was in the shade, thanks to the trees that surrounded him. From where he knelt, he could see Simone's outline in the living room window. She sat down on the edge of the sofa and hunched over something. It was now near 5:00 p.m. on Tuesday evening, and she hadn't left the house again.

She had answered none of his calls, either. He couldn't wait any longer to be closer to her. He needed to touch her. Smell her. Hear her soft voice.

Keeping low, he snuck out of the woods from behind the shed. He kept his eyes on her the whole time, but she was still hunched over something and paid no attention to the window. He dashed across the drive and up to the house. There was a smaller window to the right of the living room, and he stayed crouched down so he could peer in from the side without her seeing.

Simone slumped over her laptop. Her beautiful, stoic face was calm as ever. She gave nothing away, not even when alone. Her calmness was what intrigued him so much about her. Even as an experienced therapist, he found it impossible to read her at times. He wondered how she'd react if she knew the truth.

171

Would she react badly? What would he do then?

A coldness grabbed his stomach. He had to tell her at some point. How could they move on otherwise? It was time she knew. And it was time she told him the truth, too. He picked himself up off the ground and made his way back down into the woods to grab his car. No more hiding. Simone deserved the truth. If she was strong enough to be sneaking around and telling lies, then she could handle it.

Once he'd reached his car, he drove back up to Simone's cottage and parked up on the drive. Bracing himself against the increasing feeling he was making the wrong decision, he got out and used the spare key under the doormat to open the front door. Simone didn't know it was there, but no point hiding it now. He closed the door loudly so as not to make her jump, and called out her name.

"In here," she called back, her soft voice making his heart beat faster. She didn't sound surprised that he'd walked in without knocking. He crept through the corridor and pushed open the living room door. She hadn't moved since he'd seen her in the window.

"Hi, babe." He smiled at her and bent down to kiss her cheek. "I've missed you."

"I missed you, too." She smiled up at him and wrapped her arms around him, but her expression soon changed to sadness. "I need to talk to you."

"OK. Go on."

"I'm really sorry to do this, babe. I don't want you to think I'm ungrateful for you putting me up here, but we both need to get out of here. It isn't safe." Her eyes filled with tears.

"Of course, it's safe. You're with me. I'll stay with you if you like. What are you looking at that's scaring you?" He pointed to the laptop.

"I'm reading about that murderer, Walter Smidtts." She closed the laptop lid down and placed it on the coffee table.

"Is that why you're so scared to stay here? Because of him? He's locked away, isn't he? No need to worry about him. You need to stop reading about the case, babe."

Simone fiddled with a strand of hair that had fallen across her chest. "Well, I have something to tell you."

Theo sighed. "Me too. You go first," he said as he moved around her and took a seat on the other side of the sofa.

"Well, there was a survivor of Smidtts. Her name is Gabriella Beaufort."

Theo's stomach somersaulted, but he forced his expression into one of concern and motioned for Simone to continue.

She looked down. "I spoke to her today."

"You what?" Theo shot up from the sofa, his usual calm exterior gone. "What do you mean, you spoke to *her*? Why?"

Simone raised her hands. "Whoa, why are you so angry? I just wanted to speak to her."

He paced the living room, hands balled into fists. He tried to push past the panic in his brain and think coherently. It suddenly hit him why she'd been at the cafe. He'd seen the woman with dark hair suddenly turn and rush back to her car, but had been too busy watching Tom speak to Simone to realise who she was. Simone had gone deeper into this than he realised. No wonder she was acting so strange around him.

"Right, and what did she have to say?"

"She said Smidtts attacked her first, but the person who tried to kill her a month later was a *different* man. It wasn't Smidtts. Well, Smidtts is a murderer, but he had help. There were two of them, and one is still loose."

"What? That's insane. I read about the case, the evidence was there, and it all pointed to Smidtts. Nobody else was involved." He was shouting now, damn. He needed to stay calm. He needed to control the situation.

"Yeah, well, that's what she said. She said it was *Tom*. That maintenance worker. She saw him at the cafe today and recognised him. She's gone to the police, but he could be here right now. Please, can we just go? I don't get why you're so angry with me? I just needed to know he wouldn't come after me, but what if it was Tom who attacked me? What if he's going to get me next?" She burst into tears.

Theo said nothing for a moment. Tom? Tom Raddish, a killer? Tick wasn't capable of killing a spider for god's sake. Why the hell would Gabriella say that? Simone stared at him with tears in her eyes.

"I'm not angry at you, just at the situation," he replied quickly, his voice calmer. "You can't keep focusing on what happened to you. Or on Smidtts. It's not healthy. I mean, of course Tom didn't try to kill Gabriella. Don't you see how ridiculous that sounds?"

"But that's what she said, Theo! And he's always creeped me out. I can't imagine he gets many dates. He smells and he's dirty and has no social boundaries."

"Oh god, Simone. He's just a bit simple. He isn't dangerous at all." Theo put his head in his hands. "I thought being here would help you, but it hasn't and I don't know what else to do to fix you."

"I'm not your responsibility to fix!" Simone yelled, standing to face him. Her cheeks flushed with anger, tears gone. "And you don't even know Tom Raddish, so how would you know if he's simple or dangerous?"

"Yes, you are my responsibility!" Theo turned away, unable to look at her.

"We're partners, Theo. I'm not some little doll you need to save," she spat.

But she didn't know the truth. He looked at her sadly, his heart aching. This would be the moment he lost her. The moment she understood why she was his responsibility.

"It was me who attacked you six months ago," he whispered.

To his surprise, Simone didn't scream or run away like he'd expected. She didn't even shed a tear. Her face contorted into a cold grimace, but she looked almost triumphant.

"I know," she replied.

Simone

Simone stood firm, her bitter expression belying the myriad of emotions swirling inside her. He'd actually admitted it, finally. She'd won. Her plan worked. His face was white against his dark hair, and a tear ran down his cheek. His mouth hung open in shock.

"What did you say?" Theo stuttered.

"I know it was you," she replied in a composed voice, though her stomach was about to explode any second.

Theo looked nothing like that smiling, professional image she'd seen on his ad now. He looked more like he was about to throw up. A giggle threatened to escape, but she swallowed it back down and kept her face straight.

"You know?" he whispered.

Simone nodded slowly. Theo took a few steps back, and for a moment she thought he was going to faint, but he reached the wall and sagged against it, unable to bear his own weight.

"I don't understand?" He put his face back in his hands.

"I suspected it was you as soon as you shoved your leaflet through my letterbox. There was something familiar in your eyes. It wasn't until I met you in person that I was sure, though."

Theo's head snapped up, though his body still sagged against the wall. It was nice to see him so weak and confused. It was powerful being the one in control. This must be how he felt when he attacked her.

"You already knew when you came to me for therapy? You've known all this time?" he asked, his eyes wide and confused.

"I've known all this time," Simone confirmed. She took a seat again on the sofa, never taking her eyes off him. Her hand slipped down the gap in between the cushions, fingers curled around the thick handle of the steel blade that lay there. A far bigger blade than the hunting knife.

"But I don't understand. Why do it? Why have you been spending time with me? Why not hand me in to the police?"

"Well, like I said, I have something to tell you. Close the curtains, please." She pointed to the window behind him. Anybody could be out there without them knowing. She didn't want Tom to see them. Poor, stupid, innocent Tom. Gabriella hadn't said he attacked her at all, but it was funny to see Theo's confusion, and it got him to admit to the truth at last. Gabriella had confirmed it was Theo who tried to murder her after she spotted him on the picnic bench wearing the same hat and glasses he wore during her assault. The balaclava he wore whilst attacking Simone must be new.

She observed Theo as he moved to close the curtains without a word. It was as if he were on autopilot. Once closed, he turned to face her. His hands were balled into fists and his arms shook. For the first time, Simone felt a shiver of fear. She gripped the handle of the blade tighter. Had she gone too far, or did he really mean it when he said he loved her? Either way, it was time to find out.

Theo

Theo stared wide-eyed at Simone, his vision blurred. He forced himself to blink and rubbed his eyes again before looking back at her. Although she didn't look like his sweet Simone right now. There was a coolness to her he'd never seen. Her hand gripped something in the cracks of the sofa. Probably the damn hunting knife.

"Why haven't you told the police, then? You haven't explained," he asked. His fingernails cut into the palms of his hands. How had he not realised she knew? The very first therapy session came back to him.

"So, what specifically brings you here to see me?"

"I guess I want to know why. I want to know what makes a man feel so weak he attempts to murder an innocent woman on the street."

"You wanted to know why," he muttered.

She smiled. "Yes, well done. I wanted to know why. I nearly called the police straight away when I first saw your advert in my letterbox. It was the first thought I had. But something stopped me. A curiosity. I wanted to know what you were like in real life. Who was friends with someone like you? What made you tick? And then I found out even more about you than I wanted to know. For example, I know what you did."

She raised an eyebrow.

"What I did? I've just told you what I did. What else have I done?" Theo made sure his face gave nothing away. Simone wasn't the only one who could hide her emotions when needed.

"I know who you are, and I know you helped Smidtts," Simone replied with complete confidence in her words.

Theo couldn't help it. Helped Smidtts? It built up in his stomach, and before he could hold it back, he laughed out loud. Her face contorted into a fiery scowl, but he couldn't help it.

"You've got it all wrong. You really think I helped him? That I helped a serial killer?" Theo laughed again. No wonder she'd been lying to him, if that's what she thought.

"Well, you were there at least," Simone yelled, anger getting the better of her. "You definitely tried to kill Gabriella, because it wasn't Smidtts. She told me herself. You were in the farm car park, weren't you? Gabriella saw you watching me. She saw your reflection as she opened the door to the cafe. She mentioned nothing about Tom. I just wanted to see your reaction to it. I wanted you to admit the truth."

"Yes, yes, OK. Clearly, you've been running around doing your research behind my back. You could have just asked, you know. I would have told you. I just didn't know how to bring it up."

"And you think I did? What was I supposed to say? Oh, hi, babe. By the way, I know you tried to kill me that one time." She shook her head incredulously.

He smiled, though he couldn't remember ever feeling so sad in his life. "I was always going to tell you the truth about the assault once I knew you were strong enough to handle it."

"I've always been strong enough, Theo. Maybe you can see that now. Were you also going to tell me Smidtts is your twin brother?"

Theo wasn't sure if he was angrier at being played or impressed by her level of commitment to finding answers. "Yes. I was going to tell you it all. We are twins. Obviously not identical. He looks like Mum, and I look like Dad. This is his ring." He held up his right hand with the silver band.

She shrugged. "You do look fairly alike."

"Walter was always the funny, charming one when we were growing up. I was awkward and preferred to keep myself to myself. Our own mother thought the police arrested the wrong twin at first, for god's sake. She tried to tell the police it must have been me. Luckily, there was DNA."

"Well, he's not so charming now."

"No. He aged terribly early on, thanks to drinking and partying far too much. When he was arrested, I genuinely didn't know what to do. It devastated me. He asked me for a favour, just one. He said the evidence wasn't strong. It was all circumstantial. Except for one eyewitness."

"Gabriella Beaufort?"

Theo nodded. "When he was first taken in for questioning, they actually let him go back home. At that point, he knew about Gabriella being an issue, but he couldn't do anything about it."

"Because the police were watching him?" Simone asked.

"Yes, they watched his every move like a hawk. So, he asked me to finish her, and I stupidly agreed. I know how horrible that sounds, but Simone, I'd been with my brother my entire life. It was always us two against the world, and I was terrified of being without him. I'd do anything for those I love."

"I know that feeling," Simone stated simply. She didn't seem particularly horrified by what he was saying.

"So yes, I tried to kill Gabriella. But it turns out killing people isn't easy. I got cold feet but forced myself to push through. In the end, I couldn't go through with it, which is why she's still alive. She wriggled underneath me on the cold ground. I brought the knife up but I couldn't bring it down on her. She kicked me hard in the nuts and legged it. I didn't even get up to chase her."

"On the police report it states they found the same shoe print at the scene of her second attack?"

"Yes, I borrowed my brother's shoes. He had two pairs because he loved them so much. I loved him, but I didn't want to incriminate myself. So, I agreed to do it only if I could wear his shoes. I just wanted to save him. Maybe I could help him. I am a therapist."

The pair fell silent, each lost in their thoughts. All plausible scenarios ran through Theo's mind. She might call the police; Gabriella would certainly call them to say she saw him in the cafe. But the police had never been too interested in her story. They wanted someone to blame who was easy to find, so they blamed Walter.

"Why did you want to save someone like that? He's a monster." Simone broke the silence.

"He's my brother. My twin. I don't know how to describe the feeling of being a twin your whole life, and suddenly you're alone. It's terrifying, Simone."

"Who's Mark?"

"Who?"

"Smidtts said his friend Mark told him to do all those bad things to women." She eyed him suspiciously.

"Oh, he's always said that. I don't know. His imaginary friend, I guess? He's not exactly sane, Simone. He's been unwell for years. We didn't have the best childhood, and all the drink and drugs really messed him up. He hears voices, sees things, and has bad thoughts. He's the real reason I studied to become a therapist. I couldn't give a shit about our mother."

"But you never hurt those women apart from Gabriella? Despite being his twin? Despite having the same childhood?"

Theo stared her straight in the eye. "No, I didn't help him. I don't hear voices or see imaginary friends like he does."

"Then why did you hurt me, Theo?"

He didn't think it was possible to feel more heartache, but her voice was so small and sad that the pain was unbearable. This was the part he'd dreaded the most. His most horrid secret, and it had the potential to break the one woman he loved. He looked into her wide eyes, and he knew he had to tell her, no matter what the consequences. He had to put her out of her misery.

Simone

Simone felt more under control as she watched Theo unravel before her eyes. She stared at him, her hand still gripped around the knife. A part of her felt he would never hurt her. But that part was a liar, because he already had. Despite the care he'd shown her the last couple of months, she was unsure whether she could trust him. He took a step towards her, and she raised a hand to stop him.

"No, not yet," she said.

He nodded and dropped his head. He looked pretty pathetic standing there feeling sorry for himself.

"I just ... I don't know why I hurt you. Well, I do. But I don't know how to explain." He focused on the floor as he spoke. He didn't even have the gumption to look her in the eye. "I knew what my brother had done, but I couldn't understand why he'd done it. We'd been so close our whole lives. And always understood each other. We finished each other's sentences, knew what mood the other was in with one look, and often knew what the other was thinking before they even did."

"That sounds nice," Simone muttered, wondering how differently life would have been with no parents if she'd had a twin sister.

"It was. Until I couldn't understand what he did to those

girls. It felt like I didn't know him at all. And I wanted to know what he felt; I wanted to understand. But when I tried to hurt Gabriella, it went horribly wrong, and I didn't get it at all."

"So, you didn't enjoy hurting her?"

"What? No, of course not! But when I saw you in the bar that night." He paused and shook his head softly, lost in the memory. "You were so beautiful. I wanted you instantly when I saw you in that bar, throwing away a shot while nobody was looking. And without thinking, I was following you outside. It was as if the perfect opportunity fell into my lap and the world was trying to tell me to give it another go or something. It just happened. I didn't plan it."

He finally raised his head and looked at her. A stony silence followed. There wasn't much to say to that.

"So, you did it because you felt like it at the time. That's the big explanation?"

"I swear I felt terrible after. I have done so ever since."

"Please don't tell me how this has made you feel," Simone snapped.

He raised his hands. "Sorry, sorry. I'm not looking for sympathy, or even empathy, I just wanted to explain. I felt so bad. I heard some voices as I was about to bring down the knife, and it sort of shook me out of a daydream. And thanks to the guilt eating me up inside about what I did, I came back to you the following night. It impressed me to see your strength. But I knew you also needed some help. So, I put those leaflets through your door. I wanted you to come to me. I wanted to help you."

"That's fucking sick." Simone scoffed.

"Is it? I was trying to make amends. I wanted to put right what I'd done."

184

"Then why didn't you hand yourself in?" Simone's voice broke, and the tears finally escaped.

"And what good would that be to you? This way I can help you. I can be there for you. I truly love you, Simone. And if you want me to hand myself in, I will. Is that why you got to know me?"

She shook her head and took a deep breath, swallowing away further tears. "I wanted to know why you did it. And I wanted to hurt you."

Simone lifted her hand and showed him the knife. The blade was five inches long and had a brand-new shimmer to it. Her eyes ran across the length of the blade. She thought about how it would feel to push the blade into soft human skin. Would it be like cutting into jelly? Or would it be more difficult than that?

"I won't stop you," Theo said, staring at the knife. "I know I deserve it."

Simone lowered it, but kept her grip tight. "The thing is, Theo, I have fallen for you. I think I love you, too. This version of you, who is strong and protective and would do anything for me. But then you left that note, and you pretended to go to Ireland. You ripped my bike tyre and then repaired it. I've seen you watching me outside. Why would you do that?"

His face dropped, and a realisation hit her. All this sneaking around, and he really was stupid enough to think she knew nothing. It was laughable. As if she didn't notice him rolling around right outside her window like a goddamn army wannabe. Who did he think left the bike shed unlocked before she went out?

"The note was stupid, but you lied straight to my face about being stabbed and I was so frustrated that you wouldn't open up to me. I didn't stab you. You know that, and I know that. So yes, I got another knife and left it there. I wanted you to admit you'd stabbed yourself somehow. I lied about going to Ireland so you'd know I wasn't around and the note couldn't be from me. I had to make you see that I'm the only person who's always here for you. I will protect you. You need me, Simone, like I need you."

Simone tried to work her thoughts through the mist of confusion. "You left the knife to get me to open up to you?"

Theo nodded. "Yes. I've been desperate to know why you lied. Why did you stab yourself in the leg? I never would have stabbed you, even then. You could have died."

"Have you seen the worthless sentences men get for violence against women? Rapists and domestic abusers get barely over five years inside, and even people like your brother have it easy in a cushy psychiatric hospital. I wanted you to go down for attempted murder, at least. And a stab wound is more likely to achieve that."

She wanted to laugh at Theo's stunned face, but kept a stoical glower instead.

"Jesus, Simone," he said eventually. "You're even more fantastic than I realised. You know that? I'm not even sure you do need me."

She looked him up and down. He was such a mess. How could he think she needed him? He was the broken one. He was lost without his twin. She realised that now, and she knew what she needed to do to make everything go away.

"Listen, let's make a promise to each other. No more games. No more lies. I don't want to hurt you." Tears welled in her eyes and she put a hand up to wipe them away, finally letting go of the knife. "I really love you despite everything."

186

Theo sniffed away his own tears. "How can someone as perfect as you love someone like me?"

A heaviness sat on her heart. She'd always known she'd have to reveal her darkest secrets to Theo if they were going to work. One more confession and they'd be OK.

"I'm not as innocent as I look, Theo. And I'm certainly not perfect. I'm a murderer, just like Walter."

Theo scoffed. "Don't be ridiculous, Simone. What do you mean, you're a murderer?"

"Years ago, as a teen, I hit a teenaged boy with my car." A sob escaped. She took a deep breath as the memory came flooding back. "They died."

"Oh, babe. That's not the same thing. I'm sure it was horrible, but it's not murder. Were you driving too fast or something?"

She nodded. "I was driving far too fast. He'd broken my heart, and my dad was murdered for no reason just a few months before. I saw him die. I told the police who did it, and the police ignored me. That person wasn't punished, why would I be? So, I aimed the car right at him."

Theo's jaw hung open, but he quickly recovered and composed himself. "You killed him on purpose?"

"I didn't think he would die. I just wanted to hurt him like he hurt me. But now he's dead. So, you see, we're both fucked up. I think that's partly why we found each other, Theo. You've lost your best friend in Walter, and I've lost mine in Kerry. She's never coming out of that hospital. I know that, really. You and I deserve each other. We understand each other in a way no one else will. And if you love me too, then I want us to be a family. I think we'd make a perfect family."

Theo didn't speak for a moment. His brow wrinkled in confusion, and he looked away. "You want us to be a family?"

"Yes, Theo." Simone beamed at him, her eyes dry of tears now. She could finally share the news. She'd been desperate to tell someone ever since she found out. "I'm pregnant."

His head shot up so quickly that it banged against the wall. "Pregnant? You're pregnant?"

Simone nodded. "I'm about six weeks along, and I need to decide on whether to keep it."

She chuckled at his shocked face – his excitement turning into the widest grin she'd ever seen. He scrambled to his knees and crawled over to her, his hands clasped together as if in prayer.

"Simone, please, let us be a family. I would never hurt anyone ever again after the hell I've put you through. It's killed me. All I wanted to do was make it up to you, and this is my chance. You don't even have to work. I'll pay for everything and we can live out in the middle of nowhere, just us. Let me take care of you and the baby. We don't need anyone else. We'll be a proper family." He shuffled his knees and moved towards her, but she brandished the knife and he stopped mid shuffle. He put his hands in the air. "I won't hurt you. I promise with all my heart."

"I know you won't, because I have another secret to confess to. Just in case you're ever tempted to change your mind or trick me. Because trust is a tricky thing to regain once it's gone, and it will take me time to trust you fully."

He unclasped his hands and held them in the air. "Anything for you, babe."

"Kerry knows if anything happens to me, she has to open a safe only she knows the location of. Inside the safe is a note confirming you attacked me with a DNA sample I took when you were sleeping. Did you know the police have a sample of your blood from the busted lip you got when you attacked me?"

Theo opened his mouth but said nothing. She left him a moment to process the information, but he still didn't move or say anything at all. There was no DNA, but he seemed to believe her.

"Theo, if anything happens to me, you will go to prison. Do you understand?"

He closed his mouth and nodded. "Does Kerry know what's inside?"

"No, she thinks I'm having hallucinations and I'm paranoid. But she also thinks you will look after me, being a therapist and all."

"I will, Simone. I will make it my life's mission, OK? We can live here in this cottage. Mum owes me one. She will sell it to me for nothing." He stood and gripped her in a vice like hug as she giggled and finally let go of the knife. But she pushed him away.

"Wait! I know you'll look after us, because I'm going to make sure of it." She winked up at him. "But first, you need to do one more thing or it won't work."

"Anything for my baby's mother." He grinned.

"One, I want this cottage in my name. We can change it to joint ownership when the baby's here and I trust you again."

"OK. Done. I just need a few days to get the documents."

"Do it quickly. Because two, your brother was right, babe. Loose ends won't do, and I'm not having my baby's father dragged off to prison. We need to do something about Gabriella Beaufort."

189

Theo

The following month, nerves fluttered in Theo's stomach worse than he'd ever felt. He breathed hard and focused on the task at hand. It was an understatement to say the last time he tried to kill Gabriella it hadn't gone well. But his heart wasn't truly in it back then.

Yes, he owed it to his brother to get him out of the situation he'd dug himself into, but he hadn't really wanted to kill Gabriella. She wasn't his to kill, and it wasn't an easy job. It was messy, and then there was hiding the body. Prison was not for him. Death would be more welcome than prison.

Now, though, he had his very own family to fight for. The perfect family. He'd already signed over the cottage to Simone. It was easy enough to get his mum to sign it over. It just took some well-placed reminders that her new lover boy didn't yet know who her son was. The mere mention made her sign it over pretty quickly, and the mortgage had been paid off years ago by their arsehole of a father before he drank himself to death.

Simone told him where Gabriella worked. So currently, he sat in his inconspicuous rental car outside the Spondon school she taught in. The kids had left, but Simone found out Gabriella ran an after-school club on Thursdays. She wouldn't be out until 5:00 p.m., which was now only ten minutes away. He snapped open the camera app on his phone and checked on Simone. She was in the living room watching TV. He stroked the image of her face gently, but she stirred and threw the blanket off her.

Where was she going now? He'd told her to stay wrapped up and chill.

She moved out of the living room and his eyes hurriedly searched the other camera screens for her. He caught a glimpse of her in the corridor, and she appeared seconds later in the bathroom. Those blind spots needed sorting. He struggled to tear his eyes away as she pulled off her spaghetti strapped vest top. His hand moved inside his pants. Simone unclipped her bra and pulled down her trousers and underwear, discarding them in the corner of the bathroom. He prayed for her to turn around so he could see her bare breasts, but she turned on the shower and climbed in still facing away from him.

He groaned and forced himself to look away from her wet nakedness and drag his eyes back to the door of the school. He removed his hand from his pants, frustrated. The camera angle would have to be changed, but it was hard to hide it in the bathroom.

It impressed him how well-behaved Simone had been lately. He'd cancelled his appointments for the week so he could spend it watching her to make sure there were no more issues. She hadn't lied since the night they'd opened up to each other and admitted their darkest secrets.

They'd made a deal that would help them to repair the broken trust. She was not to lie to him again, and he was to do everything he could to protect and look after her. He'd fished that stupid Bertie Bear out of the bin to explain how badly it enraged him when she lied. That seemed to make her understand. She'd handed in her notice at that horrible rag of a newspaper, and she'd promised never to speak to Kerry again and leave her phone on the kitchen counter at night for checking. That way he could check her messages, phone calls, social media and browser history until the trust was back.

A bang rang out from the school and his head shot up. The main door to the school opened, and a group of older teenagers walked out with Gabriella right behind them. She waved them off and walked through the singular metal gate towards a bright blue Nissan Qashqai only a few cars down from Theo's Insignia. He slid down in his seat and pulled down his baseball cap. She jumped in and drove off, and Theo followed behind, making sure he stayed at least a couple of car lengths away from her.

She only drove for a few minutes before pulling left into a side street and taking another left seconds later. Theo didn't follow her on the last turn, pulling up on the side of the road instead and getting out of his car to see which driveway she had pulled on to. He spotted the Nissan a few houses down. Perfect. Now all he had to do was wait until night time.

He pulled away and drove back to his flat to prepare for the evening events. There was no need to give up the flat, despite practically living with Simone. They still needed space at times. And this was the perfect time for space. Tonight, he needed full concentration. No distractions. He filled his duffel bag with a few necessary items – rope, knife, torch – and forced himself to have a nap despite the excitement coursing through his body. There were hours to wait yet, and he needed to be sharp.

Although he'd felt bad afterwards about hurting Gabriella, he couldn't deny there had been a thrill that was like nothing he'd ever experienced before. Same again with Simone's attack. Until the guilt settled in. But this time, Simone reassured him Gabriella had no kids, no boyfriend and no family. She'd grown up in foster care. No one would miss her. She was a guilt-free treat for the night. No need for it to be quick. If he had to hide the body anyway, he may as well enjoy it, and then never do it again. And all would be fine.

He fell asleep easily in the end, thinking of what was to come.

It was around 11:00 p.m. when Theo woke up with a jolt of excitement. He grabbed his phone first to check on Simone. She was in bed and well wrapped up in the duvet. Her phone was on the kitchen counter for checking. She left it there at 10:00 p.m. each night, as they'd agreed that was late enough really. She wouldn't need a phone after that time.

It had just ticked past midnight when he drove the short distance back to Gabriella's house. Being a Wednesday evening, there was little traffic on the roads, bar one or two passing cars. All the same, Theo kept his head down whenever one passed by on the off chance it was someone he knew. He parked one street away from Gabriella's building. Not wanting to be too close to her house, or to be seen walking too far with a duffel bag in the early hours of the morning.

He grabbed the bag from the back seat and walked with his head right down. Not one person was around, no lights turned on. Once positive he was outside the correct house, he crept down the drive to the back gate. His stomach tingled with excitement as he realised the gate was unlocked. From the rear garden he could relax a little. No neighbour windows overlooked the garden, and he could pick open the back door without being seen.

He stepped over to the door, keeping his eye out for any

sudden lights from neighbours or for any movement inside Gabriella's house. But the night was eerily still. Not even a cat wandered around. He put his bag down and opened the flap to get his torch and tools, but something nagged at him to look back up.

What if...?

He carefully pulled on a pair of vinyl gloves and pulled the handle down. The back door popped open for him to walk straight inside the house. How could a lone woman be so stupid as to leave the back door unlocked? The universe had aligned for him. It was meant to be. He'd been given the perfect chance to live out a fantasy he didn't realise he had. And with no interfering and no guilt. His whole body buzzed as he stepped over the threshold of Gabriella's back door. There was no turning back now.

Simone

Simone pulled up her white T-shirt and held her stomach out in front of the full-length bedroom mirror. She rubbed a hand across the dainty hairs under her belly button before letting out her breath. She couldn't actually be showing yet at only eleven weeks. The baby was nothing but an insignificant dot of extra cells. But her stomach looked bloated all the same. Maybe it was all in her head.

She sighed and pulled her top back down, jumping onto the soft bed behind her. Her eyes flicked over once again to the clock on the bedside table. It was 01:00 a.m. He'd be inside the house soon, if not already. She swallowed down the nerves. Tonight would be over quickly, and then she could go back to enjoying her pregnancy. She thought of all the things she was going to do once they were a family. No more work. She could stay home and look after the little one. Stay-at-home mums always seemed so stressed though, so maybe not. She already missed going to work more than she'd imagined. But if they lived out in the Peak District it would be impossible to commute, anyway. There were so many questions on her mind that waiting another seven months to get an answer was torture.

What would the baby look like? Would I be a good mother?

She knew she'd be better than her own abusive arsehole of a mother. Maybe she'd be as good a parent as Dad, or better even. Hopefully she'd make him proud wherever he was. She was already willing to kill for her child. So that must be a good start.

Though the police would disagree.

She put the police out of her head. They wouldn't get caught. It's impossible. They weren't connected in any way. She'd used a fake profile to talk to Gabriella and convinced her to delete any messages, just in case. Plus, Theo would get the blame. The man always did. It was one of the few advantages women had over men. She sank back into the mattress and stretched out. She couldn't sleep until the murder was over, but she could try to at least relax until then. Stress wasn't good for the baby. She owed it to her child to stay calm.

Until she heard a door creak downstairs.

She sat up on the bed, heart pounding. One hand instinctively flew to her stomach. She sat deathly still; her ears strained through the darkness. But the house was silent once again. She stood and snuck over to the bedroom door, nudging it open an inch so she could listen.

Slow footsteps came from downstairs. Someone was inside, and they were doing their best to sneak around without being heard. She closed the door shut tight as quietly as she could. Her eyes frantically searched the room. The bed. She could hide under the bed.

She snuck over to the other side of the bed and crawled underneath. She clamped one hand over her mouth and prayed that they wouldn't find her as heavy thuds ascended the stairs.

Theo

Theo snuck inside Gabriella's house, unable to keep the wide grin off his face and peeled his ears for any noise. The house was silent. He flicked on his torch and saw that the back door had led him straight into the kitchen. He swung the light from side to side. The kitchen was tidy, save one plate left in the sink and a pair of women's trainers by the back door. A 'Live, Laugh, Love' sign was on the kitchen table, right next to a photo of Gabriella with another woman. She lived alone, judging from this room. There was no presence of a second person. No second pair of shoes or second plate.

He walked over to the photo and thumbed it gently. Gabriella was prettier than he remembered. She wore a figure-hugging little black dress in the photo, which hugged every line of her athletic body. He ran a finger over her breasts and placed the photo back down.

There was another door to his left which needed to be checked first. It led to a plain living room painted in magnolia, other than one feature wall, which was a deep tone of purple. The far wall was covered in photos. He ran the torch over them. She seemed to know lots of people, contrary to what Simone had said. He studied the images. Gabriella looked close to one older couple in particular. An uncomfortable feeling replaced his excitement.

Maybe this was a bad idea if there were people who would miss her.

He could call Simone, but the thought of it made his heart heavy. It wasn't just letting Simone and the baby down that would be awful. Simone had convinced Gabriella not to go to the police until she'd found some evidence against Theo. And Gabriella believed her. But if she didn't die soon, then she'd call the police and tell them everything. He'd end up in prison, Simone would be alone and the baby would never know him. Plus, a part of him wanted to know what it would be like. He'd wanted to know since Walter's crimes were revealed. And he would likely never get another chance.

So, he shrugged off the photos. Whether or not she had family, she had to die.

He crept through the living room and ended up in a corridor where the stairs lay. He switched off his torch in front of them to listen. The house stayed silent, so he flicked the torch back on and climbed up the steps. The third one creaked and made him stop dead in his tracks, but still there was no noise.

There were four doors at the top of the stairs. One door was straight in front of him, and wide open. He stepped over and shined his torch inside. The sharp light fell on a grey slate, then a toilet, and then a bath. He walked in to check the products on the side; they were all for a female. He opened a bottle of shampoo and sniffed. Strawberry. Maybe she'd smell like strawberries. It would be a nice memory, if so.

Two of the other doors were closed, and one was ajar by about an inch. He snuck over to the open door first and peered around it. It was dark, but he could make out a bed. And the back of Gabriella's dark head of hair on the pillow. The duvet moved gently up and down. Perfect. He watched her for a moment. She was so peaceful. No idea her life was about to end. A feeling stirred inside him. He'd always assumed it would be guilt he felt when he got closer to doing the deed, but if he was honest, he was more aroused than anything else.

The last thing he needed was a nasty surprise from a roommate, though. He closed the door once again and snuck back down the corridor to check the other two rooms. He opened the first door as silently as possible. It was a tiny room filled with boxes and suitcases. He moved over to the last door and pushed it open. He chuckled out loud. It was empty. Perfect. He and Gabriella would be uninterrupted.

He placed the duffel bag down on the floor outside Gabriella's room and took out the tape and knife. Simone had insisted he tie her up first and explained why she needed to die. She wanted him to apologise for her. He hadn't argued. The thought of Gabriella being naked and tied was more exhilarating to him than he'd let on to Simone. She didn't need to know everything. She'd be happy as long as Gabriella was out of their lives and no longer a risk to their family. Thank god he'd always been a good liar.

He snuck back inside Gabriella's room. His footsteps made soft thuds against the carpet as he walked over to her bed. He stood above her first and watched the duvet move up and down rhythmically. She held a classic beauty with her high cheekbones and strong nose. He hadn't noticed that before. Everything was over in a blur last time. He'd panicked being out in the open that someone would see them and grab him. This was much better. They'd have time alone. She might even enjoy him for a time. He stroked her soft cheek once, and her nose wrinkled.

He pulled the tab of tape back and forced it over her mouth in one smooth motion, biting off the end.

Her eyes opened wide and flashed with terror. He threw one leg over her body, trapping her under the duvet as she kicked out. The tape dulled her screams as he held it down against her mouth. He bit off the edge and threw the tape on the bed next to him. She flung her arms and bucked under his weight, but she was no match for his strength. She might be feisty, but she didn't stand a chance of getting away from him this time.

The pain of her kicking him in the balls previously came back to him. He was going to enjoy this. He pinned her arms under the duvet with his legs and closed both hands around her throat.

"Listen to me," he growled. She stopped fighting and stared up at him. Her cheeks were red, eyes wide and full of tears. Snot flew from her nose. She was a hot mess. "If you want to live, you need to do as I say. Nod if you understand."

She gave him a tiny nod, despite him holding her throat. That would do.

"Good girl. I need your arms. Do not fight me, or I will fucking kill you."

He took one hand away from her throat and showed her the knife. She nodded again, and he shifted his weight to allow her to pull her arms out. He forced both hands together, using his teeth to bite off more tape and wrapped it around her wrists. But she wriggled free and smacked him across the face. Pain seared his lip, and the metallic taste of blood made him feel nauseous.

"You stupid bitch," he growled.

He grabbed her arms again and pulled the tape around her wrists as tightly as possible. He ignored her muffled cries, brought his hand up and smacked her across the face with all his might. She groaned, her eyes rolling backwards.

"You're going to pay for that. Now, remember, you do as I say, and I won't kill you, OK?" he growled again.

She nodded slowly, still dazed from the slap. He kept the knife close to her throat and climbed off the bed, careful to monitor her the whole time. Before she had time to fight again with those damn legs, he pulled her by her hair and threw her on the floor, kicking her in the stomach to make sure she stayed down while he taped her ankles together. It delighted him to see she was naked already. She tried to writhe on the floor until he shut her up with a hard punch to the back. He moved his torch over her body. She was fully bound and couldn't make any noise. His mind was in overdrive, still enraged that this stupid cow had slapped him so hard. She had his blood on her hands now. She cried out and tried to speak through the tape; it sounded like 'please.' But he ignored her. His anger took over and his hands shook violently. There was no way she could survive.

"Listen, Gabriella." He bent down and grabbed her chin, forcing it upwards so she had to look at him. Her eyes were bloodshot and crazed. Maybe she was realising she shouldn't have slapped him, but she still needed to be punished. "I will need to punish you for hurting me. I warned you not to, but I can understand you panicked. I can forgive you, but only after punishment. Once that's done, I'll wash you and we can have some fun before you go back to bed. I'll make it nice at times for you if you behave, OK?"

Gabriella said nothing, but another sob escaped. She was so fucking ungrateful. He unzipped his trousers and dragged her onto her knees.

"Hey, babe."

He grabbed the knife and whizzed around, falling onto his back. He raised the knife high in the air. Simone stood in the doorway.

"What are you doing here?" he gasped, trying to catch his breath from the fright. Simone was in bed, wasn't she?

"I couldn't let you have all the fun, could I?" She stepped over to him, a wide smirk on her face.

Her eyes shined with excitement. It was the same glint he used to think was her vulnerability shining through. Clearly, he was wrong.

She cocked her head. "Why is she bent over like that? Are you going to fuck her?"

"No, no, of course not. I would never do—" He scrambled to his feet and turned to one side so she couldn't see his unzipped trousers. "Wait, you want to join in with killing her?" he asked incredulously.

"It wouldn't be my first rodeo. I told you about Micky Suave, right? I may have forgotten to mention my mother. Her death may also have been more my fault than I cared to admit to you." She winked.

Gabriella cried out once more, and Simone rushed over and booted her in the stomach. She flipped Gabriella over onto her back and straddled her face as the woman bucked underneath her. Theo's stomach dropped. What the hell was she doing? His sweet Simone didn't act this way.

"I'm not sure she can breathe. Shall I suffocate her?"

"No!" he hissed. "Simone, what about the baby? I told you to wait at home. We said no more lies, remember?"

"But I want to join in." She pouted and pushed herself off Gabriella's face. "Don't you see? This will bond us for life.

There's no turning on each other if we both join in. I want to do this for you. For us. For our family."

Theo's shoulders relaxed. It was his sweet Simone. Of course, she was just doing this for them. Gabriella let out another sob, and Simone stood to meet him. Christ, she was sexy. She gripped the handle of the knife in his hands.

"I'll hold this while you fuck her first. Hurry." She grinned in a way he'd never seen her do before.

He gulped and allowed her to take the knife. In that moment, he knew he was the luckiest man in the world to have this gorgeous woman on his side. And not just on his side, but the actual mother of their children. Gabriella's muffled screams called to him, and he glanced down at her. He then bent down to finish what he'd started with Simone now watching. She stepped back over to Gabriella's face and sat down on it once more.

"Hurry, before she suffocates." There was that grin again.

Hmm. Maybe this was too much. He was flaccid now. If Simone was just doing this for them, why was she so goddamn happy about it? Did she get a kick from hurting people? Maybe it was Simone who needed to be punished, but his baby was still inside, so no pain. Isolation would be good. A locked room with a camera to make sure she was OK, of course. He wasn't a monster. An ache in his groin told him he was getting hard again, and he grabbed Gabriella's legs to lift them both onto one shoulder. But he lost his breath and dropped her legs. A sharp pain caused his hand to fly to his chest. His shirt was soaking wet. Sweat?

Breathing was hard, he gasped in and out. Fear gripped him, and his eyes widened like Gabriella's had been moments ago. He peered down at her; Simone was gone. Gabriella didn't look scared anymore. Hands pushed him backwards onto the floor, and he stared up at Simone.

"Babe?" he whispered, looking back up at Simone. Her face was stony. The knife was no longer in her hands. He looked down, and there it was, sticking out of his own chest.

"Yes, babe?" Simone answered.

He tried to reach out to her to explain she needed to stop. The knife was in his chest. She needed to help him. But his arms were weak and he could barely lift them to get her attention. His breath came in heavy gasps. It was OK. It would be fine. Simone would realise soon and call an ambulance, and it would all be OK.

He blinked, and his vision blurred. Simone ripped open the duct tape on Gabriella's arms and mouth. She must be telling Gabriella it was a joke or something, so she could call the ambulance for him. That made sense. Can't call an ambulance when you're in the middle of murdering someone.

Gabriella spluttered and panted, but instead of running, she turned around to lie on her back. She had stopped crying – her face now set in a hard grimace.

"I'm ready," Gabriella said, giving Simone a nod.

"Come here, babe." Simone grabbed him by the shoulder and helped him to his knees. Thank god. She was finally going to help him.

His mouth filled with liquid. Sick? No, the metallic taste meant it was blood. He spluttered and tried to spit it out. He had to tell Simone. She needed to know he couldn't breathe.

"I can't—"

"Shhhh, babe. I know," Simone interrupted.

Simone's hands dug into his shoulders, and his weight shifted up.

"Come on, babe, help me get you up."

OK. Simone was trying to get him to safety. He tried to stand, and suddenly he was in the air, but not for long as he fell on top of Gabriella, whose eyes were firmly closed.

Had Simone killed her?

Gabriella's skin felt so soft and warm. The smell of strawberry shampoo stuck in his nostrils from her hair, and her heart beat rapidly fast under his cheek. She wasn't dead, then.

"Did you really think I was going to let you anywhere near my baby? You chose the wrong women to carry out your sick fantasies on, Theo *Mark* Smidtts."

Simone? She sounded so angry.

"I know it was you who made your brother do all that sick stuff. Too scared to live out your own fantasies." Simone's voice continued, but it was echoing as though she was far away. "And now you'll die at the hands of your victims. Us."

The realisation of her betrayal made his chest ache more than the knife. His Simone had stabbed him on purpose. She'd chosen Gabriella over him? He tried to speak but spluttered blood.

"That's probably enough blood on you, Gabriella. Push him off in that direction where there's already blood, and leave him where he lands naturally. Then call the police, and I'll go now and get out of here."

He tried to move his arms again, but they were too weak. The room dimmed, though the light was still on. He felt Gabriella move out from under him, and suddenly his head was against the carpet. *That's why the back door was open*, he thought as his eyes closed and the silence came.

Simone

The following summer, Simone sat in the nursery of her brand-new four-bed, detached house nestled in the middle of Buxton. Where better to bring up children than a spa town surrounded by natural beauty? And with no serial killer lair in sight, thank god.

She could smile now when she thought of Theo. He was gone forever. It had been difficult at times to stay close enough to him to draw him in, but she'd needed to be certain before killing him. Unlike him and his brother, she'd never kill someone who didn't deserve it. As soon as she was sure Theo was as bad as his brother, he'd been fair game. And what he was about to do to Gabriella proved how evil he was. Never mind how controlling he'd tried to be with Simone.

He was nothing but a means to an end, anyway. So, the cottage was sold as soon as Theo was dead. The little cottage sold for half a million quid thanks to its location and land, meaning she could easily afford to live wherever she wanted.

She picked up Zoe from the crib and rested her own cheeks against Zoe's tiny, chubby ones, breathing in the sweet scent of her scalp. She always smelled so amazing. Simone could have sniffed her all day. Weird, but true. Being a parent was strange at times.

She'd realised that pretty quickly. You do things you never thought of before. Not things like murdering their dad, but sniffing another person's butt is completely normal as a parent. And as for love, any other feeling paled compared to the love of a child. She sat down and took out a breast for Zoe to latch onto. Despite the weirdness, being a mother was better than she could have ever imagined.

Her own mother crossed her mind as she ran a finger up and down Zoe's dimpled thigh. Simone was going to be so much better than that murdering bitch. The memory of her stabbing her father was one she'd never forget. The police didn't take her witness testimony seriously. She'd told them all about the times her mother had been violent towards him, but her mother, but they didn't believe her. She might have been believed today, but it happened twenty years ago. As if a woman would violently abuse her husband, never mind kill him.

They hadn't believed a word Simone told them and believed her mother when she said her poor dad was the aggressor. The revenge of emptying pill after pill into her mother's drink, on the other hand, was one of her best memories. If there was one thing she could thank her mother for, it was for teaching her how to be strong when necessary. Where people deserved it, anyway.

As Zoe gurgled her milk, baby Gabriella called out from the crib. Simone glanced over. The baby lay on her back, cooing at the ceiling and mesmerised by the lights. She'd named her after the special lady who helped them to get away from Daddy for good. Sometimes she still couldn't believe Gabriella agreed to the plan. But she hadn't taken as much convincing as Simone expected. They had more in common than she thought possible, which was partly related to why Gabriella ended up in foster care. Her own mother wasn't much better than Simone's.

Gabriella and Kerry were the only people who knew where Simone and the twins lived, as well as DI Swanson. He'd visited twice last year to keep her updated on the original case. Gabriella had informed Swanson that Theo was the one who attacked her originally, and he'd come back to finish her off. The police agreed Gabriella acted in self-defence in stabbing Theo with his own knife. The one he'd brought with him to kill her. It's not like she was lying. It was self-defence.

And although it wasn't proven in court, DI Swanson believed it was Theo who had attacked Simone, and he would likely have killed her, too. It had helped that she'd planted a seed in Swanson's head previously by making sure he knew Theo was acting weird whenever anything strange happened in the holiday home the previous spring. The police had found all her things in his flat – despite his texts to her confirming they were in a storage unit. And they found a camera app on his phone, confirming he'd been watching Simone's every move. But Simone knew that already. Theo wasn't as clever as he thought he was.

"Where are you, babe?" a voice called from the hallway and broke Simone's thoughts.

"In here," Simone called back.

Kerry walked into the bedroom, a grin on her face as usual. Simone's heart fluttered. Kerry was wearing her own silk pyjamas, and she looked extremely sexy with her ruffled bedhead. Simone cradled Zoe tighter and stood to walk over to Kerry. She planted a kiss on her cheek, and Kerry kissed Zoe's forehead. The baby giggled and unlatched from Simone's nipple.

"Come here, baby. Come to Mammy," Kerry said as she took Zoe. The little one squealed in delight at seeing her.

Though they did most parenting tasks equally, other than breastfeeding, Zoe seemed to prefer Kerry and had a similar, loud personality to her. Whilst the opposite was true of baby Gabriella, who was far more like Simone. They'd make a fantastic pair when they were older. No one would mess with either of them.

"Love you." Simone squeezed Kerry's hand and stepped over to the cot to pick up Gabriella. She kissed her head softly and Gabriella nestled into her arm. Content and sleepy. She snapped a picture with her phone to send to her namesake. They'd be seeing Gabriella tomorrow, and Simone couldn't wait.

"Love you, too." Kerry beamed back.

Kerry was the only other person who knew the full story of what had happened with Theo. And with Kerry by her side, Simone knew the twins would grow into amazing human beings despite their DNA. Getting pregnant was the greatest part of the plan. What better way to get back at Theo? He stole her sense of safety, independence, and strength. So, she'd taken from him the one thing he desperately wanted. And the girls couldn't *not* be amazing being surrounded by such powerful role models.

She'd almost felt sorry for Theo in the end. He didn't stand a chance against two women like Gabriella and her. But then again, he deserved to pay for what he did. And you should never underestimate a scorned woman.

Sure, she could have put him in prison, but he'd be out in a few years with the useless sentences thugs got these days.

And then, no doubt, he'd be looking for custody of the girls. Not long before his death, she'd seen a violent thug murder his partner in cold blood, and yet he was still allowed to have access to their babies. Simone would never allow that to happen to her twins.

Death was the only thing that would keep him away from the babies. His ring now lay in her grandmother's trinket box, next to Micky Sarve's nose ring, her mother's brooch and her aunt's necklace. The trinket box was now hidden inside a sewn-up Bertie Bear. Her family was never there for her since dad died. But now she had her own family, and they were where her priority lay now. And god help anyone who ever tried to hurt them, she thought as she sat back down in the nursery chair to feed Gabriella.

Kerry wandered off laughing with Zoe. So Simone picked up the book she'd decided it was time to read, 'Little Women'. She fingered the inscription from her dad, before turning to page one and settling into the chair.

Also by Ashley Beegan

Lucy's Coming...

Summer Thomas questions her own sanity when violent patient, Lucy Clark, disappears from a locked hospital ward.

Because no one else will admit that Lucy exists.

As Summer digs deeper into the disappearance, it becomes apparent that Lucy is looking for her too, but Summer should have stayed away. Now, Lucy is coming for her...

And there's no escaping someone who doesn't exist.

Mother... Liar... Murderer?

'The truth you must tell,
* To all who you know,*
* Or you'll end up in hell,*
* Where you'll never grow.'*

Eleven years ago, Astrid Moor got away with **murder.** Now, someone wants to make her pay.

Astrid turns to Alex Swanson for help, the officer who risked everything for her once before. Except he's a big shot DI now, and isn't prepared to help her again.

But even though she's alone, Astrid doesn't take kindly to threats, and when she finally realises who is terrorising her she makes a decision she will never recover from.

A decision with far worse consequences than any secrets from her past.

The Hospital

'The dogs always bark,
* And the violets die a death,*
* When the devil brings the dark,*
* And when he gets inside my head.'*

ASHLEY BEEGAN

Summer Thomas is fighting for her life after coming face to face with the devil of Adrenna Psychiatric Hospital.

So it's up to DI Alex Swanson to find out the truth behind the hospital and what happened to her, and he needs to be quick if he wants to save others from meeting the same fate.

But Swanson has his own health scare and past demons are back to haunt him. With the devil close by, he might not survive long enough to save anyone. As the history of the hospital becomes clear, he needs to figure out who he can trust to tell him the truth.

Before he ends up meeting the devil himself.

The Confession

When a dishevelled man walks into Derbyshire police station and admits to murdering over four hundred people, the entire East Midlands Special Operations Unit jumps into action.

DI Alex Swanson is suspicious of this soft spoken murderer, Billy Bailey. He doesn't look capable of murdering one person, never mind hundreds. Even if he did, why does he suddenly want to confess?

But why would anyone lie about being a murderer?

As the body count grows, it appears Billy Bailey is at least telling the truth about where his long list of victims ended up. But when another young woman disappears whilst Billy is still in custody, Swanson's suspicions grow. He digs deeper and reveals a horrifying network of lies and deceit far too close to home.

It's a web he needs to unravel before time runs out, or yet another young woman will be taken from her family for good.

Made in the USA
Monee, IL
31 July 2022